MW01243556

THE SOUND OF VICTORY

Sometimes all you've got to do to get even
is let someone blindly run into what they deserve.

By Jim Stovall

Motivational PRESS®
LEADERS IN GLOBAL PUBLISHING

Published by Motivational Press, Inc.
7777 N Wickham Rd, # 12-247
Melbourne, FL 32940
www.MotivationalPress.com

Manufactured in the United States of America.

ISBN: 978-1-62865-131-7

Contents

This book is dedicated to the fans and friends
of Jacob, Monica, and Franklin.
Thank you for keeping their story and my dreams alive.

"A man may see how this world goes
with no eyes.
Look with thine ears:
See how yond justice rails
upon yond simple thief."
William Shakespeare

Chapter One

It was more than just a baseball game. Yes, indeed. It was the first baseball game of a brand new season.

This is an annual rite of passage only fully understood by certain enlightened individuals who appreciate the complexities and intricacies of our national pastime.

I was enjoying opening day as my beloved St. Louis Cardinals were taking on the godless Chicago Cubs in St. Louis's Busch Stadium. It's not that the Chicago Cubs, in and of themselves, are particularly godless. It is quite simply that anyone who dares to compete against the Cardinals —at least in my mind—becomes instantly godless.

I was enjoying opening day in my favorite, and in what has become my traditional, spot. That would be on the terrace outside my 22nd floor apartment in the Plaza Tower building. Many uninitiated individuals would wonder why my terrace is the preferred spot for opening day instead of a box seat behind home plate in Busch Stadium. While the Plaza Tower apartment building, where I have become a permanent fixture, boasts a great view, it does not overlook Busch Stadium. As a matter of fact, it is at least 350 miles away from St. Louis, located along the Arkansas River in Tulsa, Oklahoma.

My name is Jacob Dyer; Jake to my friends and *that blind guy in the St. Louis Cardinals hat and Albert Pujols jersey* to those who don't know me.

As I sat on my terrace with my traditional Cardinal wardrobe and my specially designed radio receiver with the illegal antenna, I could clearly hear the broadcast on the radio beaming out from St. Louis. The legendary play-by-play announcer was calling the game just as he has done since I was a Little Leaguer in grade school more than 30 years ago. His voice occasionally falters these days, but so do my ears.

As I sat there enjoying my frigidly cold beer and my hoarded double Corona Dominican Republic cigar which I had been anticipating for months waiting for opening day, all was indeed right with the world. My masterpiece from the Dominican Republic was handcrafted by an artisan beyond compare, and its double Corona length assures one that, if enjoyed judiciously, it will take you through an entire 9-inning ballgame. Some things are just meant to be.

My Cardinals got off to a typical start and were trailing five to three in the sixth inning. This does not concern us Cardinal fans as much as it used to before the saint himself, known as Albert Pujols, arrived on the scene. Sir Albert gives us all hope that at any point in time, with one swing of his mighty bat, the Cardinals can be propelled instantly back into the thick of things.

As the announcer and the able color analyst, a former Cardinal legend himself, painted the picture for me, the bottom of the sixth was off to a good start. The Red Birds got two men on with only one out, and the roar from the stadium could be felt in Tulsa as Pujols strode to the plate.

At that very instant, the portable telephone that I keep on my terrace, for some reason that escaped me at that moment, rang shrilly. I instantly leapt to my feet, picked up the phone, and turned it off, leaving the caller to deal with my answering machine or any other infernal device that should confront those without enough sense to know not to be calling on opening day in the bottom of the sixth inning with Albert batting and representing the go-ahead run.

As I sipped what was no longer my first, second, or third cold beer and puffed on my Dominican dream, I dismissed the annoying caller by allowing that some people did not have the benefit of a proper upbringing.

It was, indeed, the stuff of which legends are made. As the announcer intoned, "Two balls and two strikes as the Cub hurler faces Pujols. And now the windup and the pitch is on the way."

The crack of the bat sounded like the shot heard 'round the world, or at least all the way from St. Louis to Tulsa. The broadcast team, being consummate professionals, did not talk over the sound of the bat and let the crowd noise fill the airwaves. Then the announcer simply said, "That one is all the way out of here!"

As he described Pujols rounding the bases, I tipped my cap, puffed on my cigar, and toasted number 5 with my latest cold beer.

Finally, the crowd settled down, and as the game was resuming, I could hear the telephone inside my apartment ringing again, but as the portable on the terrace was already silenced, I dealt with the problem by increasing the volume on the radio slightly and sitting back to enjoy the final three innings. I knew the caller had to be either another unenlightened pagan who did not realize it was opening day or someone calling to inform me of Pujols's heroics in which I was already reveling.

Albert's blast proved to be the game-winner as the Cardinals bested the Cubs 6 to 5 on opening day. If life gets any better than this, I simply fail to recognize it.

As I listened to the post game interviews, I continued to contemplate the promise of a new season and everything in life I held sacred. Little did I know that one of the casually dismissed phone calls would lead me on an odyssey of discovery and affirm the things in my life that truly are sacred.

Chapter Two

That was the year that I became known as the Midnight Runner. I never intended to pick up this moniker, but, as often happens, the name stuck to me and probably always will.

All of us are born with endless possibilities and great expectations. Then slowly, but inevitably, we begin to understand our own looming mortality and increasing limitations.

I remember being an eleven-year-old Little League baseball player when I was absolutely sure that it was just a matter of time until I took my place in center field for the beloved St. Louis Cardinals. This was not arrogance or pride on my part. It was simply the way the world orders itself in the mind of an eleven-year-old boy.

That summer, our Little League team was really good. Our fielders had pretty good gloves, the bats were starting to come around as they will when the teenage years approach, and we actually had one pitcher who could make the baseball do things that none of us had ever seen before. In the first few years of Little League baseball, pitchers are doing well if they can launch the ball in the general direction of the batter and hit the backstop.

Somehow over the winter months, my boyhood friend Ed Willard's arm had undergone a transformation, and his pitches began to curve, dive, and dance around the plate. This made batting practice difficult for our team but was a joy as we watched all of the other teams in the league struggle with this new phenomenon.

Then came the day that we played our rivals from Marshall Elementary School. We had played them several times each season since we started

Little League baseball, so no one thought much about it. But when they took the field, their center fielder looked like someone's dad or at least their older brother. The umpire actually questioned the opposing coach but was assured the center fielder was under twelve years old.

Everyone doubted this as, without a birth certificate in evidence, one had to hang suspicions on the fact that the lad in question needed a shave. When he got up to bat, despite the newly found prowess of Ed Willard, Marshall's center fielder hit the ball farther than anyone in our league had ever seen. To this day, all anyone could attest to is the fact that the ball was still climbing as it went over the fence and out of sight. For all I know, that baseball may still be going.

As an eleven-year-old, I felt the first slight crack in my armor of certainty that I was destined to play center field for the St. Louis Cardinals. A year later, I gave up baseball completely when I realized that football was better suited to my natural talents.

I had a very respectable, if not distinguished, high school football career and could have probably played at a small college somewhere if Uncle Sam had not been in tremendous need of my skills and talent in Vietnam.

My marginal athletic prowess got me through basic training easier than most of the other guys, and I had never thought about my body not being able to do anything I wanted it to until my helicopter was hit over a Southeast Asian jungle, and my best friend, John Ivers, miraculously got us out of the kill zone and somehow crash landed our chopper on the deck of a hospital ship in the China Sea.

That's when I began the journey that took me from a carefree youth to a point where I knew I would live the rest of my life as a blind person if I decided to live the rest of my life.

As too quickly happens, the years multiplied like Oklahoma jackrabbits, and before I knew it, I was almost middle-aged. The term *middle-aged* is like one of those mirages that sometimes can be seen as you are driving on a long, hot, flat stretch of highway. The cool water appears to be at a spot just ahead of you, but somehow, when you get there, it is just a bit farther off in the distance. For the past decade or so, I had been thinking I was only a few years from middle age.

Those of us of the male persuasion are eternally blessed and cursed with an element we politely call ego. Among other things, this male ego tells us that with just a little bit of training, attention to our diet, and the moderation of some questionable habits, we can be in playing shape again and ready to kick off another season. Deep down, we may know this is not true, but the farther along the road we go, the less we are inclined to look deep down.

Since I was not willing to negotiate with respect to my predilection for gourmet food, fine wine, late nights, cold beer, and blessed cigars, I thought I might turn back the hands of time with just a bit of physical exercise.

Near the Plaza building where I live, along the banks of the Arkansas River, there is a bicycle trail often used as a jogging or walking path that seemed perfect for me to put in my roadwork and begin counting up the miles as a part of my new fitness program. The only thing wrong with the plan was that I was an out-of-shape almost middle-aged blind guy; but it didn't stop me from becoming known as the Midnight Runner.

Chapter Three

As I cleared the debris from my terrace that was left over after the Cardinals' game, I continued to bask in the glow of an opening day victory. I wanted to get everything on the terrace just right, because the next day was Saturday and that meant a double-header with the godless Cubs. Everything in life seemed to be going my way.

Inside my apartment, I slipped into a light jacket, got out my white cane, and prepared to walk to my office. I locked the door to my apartment and rang for the elevator.

It is a mere eight blocks across the edge of downtown Tulsa to my office in the Derrick Building. I enjoy the walk at all hours of the day and night, with the possible exception of morning and evening rush hours. During that time, there are too many people crowded onto the sidewalk for me to feel comfortable.

But as it was about 7:30 on a Friday evening, downtown Tulsa was like a ghost town. It's a bustling place during business hours Monday through Friday, but clears out instantly evenings and weekends. I enjoy downtown Tulsa while everyone else is enjoying their evenings and weekends in the suburbs.

As a blind person walking with the aid of my white cane, I always experience a flood of emotions. First of all, the cane and I have a perpetual love-hate relationship. I love being independent and hate having to use it. Once I get past that, I can enjoy all of the sounds, smells, and textures of the city.

As I rounded the last corner and approached the Derrick Building, I heard the familiar voice of my friend and newsstand proprietor, Leroy Small.

"How 'bout those Cardinals, Jake? A perfect season. You should pray for another players' strike."

Leroy is a Yankee's fan. I have always considered myself to be open-minded, tolerant, and willing to overlook imperfections in those around me. Leroy has never appreciated the sacrifice I have to make with respect to his New York Yankees.

I said, "Well, I guess you expect your Yankees to win another pennant."

Leroy laughed and called back, "I wouldn't have it any other way, Jake. Are you going to work all night?"

"No rest for the weary," I replied.

Actually, daylight and dark do not hold the same standard restrictions in my world that they seem to have for sighted people. I went through the revolving door and entered the ornate lobby of the Derrick Building.

The Derrick Building is a massive marble masterpiece that was built during the Depression when people in Oklahoma had more oil and money than judgement and brains. I love it because it's one of a kind and could never be replicated.

I pushed the button for the elevator and heard the antique mahogany doors slide open. Inside the elevator, I pushed the button for the 14th floor. Sighted tenants in the building always wonder how I can find the right button. It's simple. It's in the same place every time.

The elevator rumbled and creaked up the shaft in a familiar and comforting way. Those glass and aluminum elevators that feel like a space shuttle launch make me nervous.

The faithful elevator deposited me on the 14th floor, and I made my way to the last door at the end of the corridor where I know the sign on the frosted glass reads *Dyer Straits Lost and Found*. I used my key and entered the lobby.

I crossed into my corner office, eased into my familiar leather chair, leaned back, and opened the window behind me. None of that re-circulated air here in the Derrick Building, but instead real live windows that open. For those of us who live in the dark, windows that let in the spring breeze are much more valuable than those that offer some dubious view.

I picked up my phone and called my answering machine back at the apartment to find out who had called during the baseball game and what could possibly motivate someone to perform such an insane act. I had refrained from checking while at my apartment, because I felt that anyone who was willing to call at such an inopportune time, therefore violating the recognized law of the universe, should wait a bit longer for me to call them back.

As I heard the answering machine engage on the other end of the line, I entered my security code and heard the first message play back.

"Jake, this is Billy Jack. I don't hardly know what to say. I would have lost everything if it wasn't for you. I would pay five times the fee we agreed on."

I heard the machine beep, signaling the end of my first message.

Here at the Dyer Straits Lost and Found Agency, we do, quite simply, what the name implies. We help people find what they have lost. We're not police, we're not private detectives, we're not an insurance company, nor investigators. But when someone falls through all of those cracks, they usually end up here. Those who have never used our service often find it humorous that people pay a lot of money to a blind man to help them find something or recover something they have lost. Billy Jack is a classic example of what we do.

As I sat with my feet propped up on my antique desk, I mentally forgave him for calling during the baseball game.

Billy Jack Johnson thinks that football is the only sport in the world. We met at Riverside High School here in Tulsa well over 25 years ago. We actually made the varsity team together our first year in high school. To say that Billy Jack and I were on the same team does not, in fact, mean that our talent was in the same league or even the same universe.

I had thought I was a great football player, destined for stardom. Then I saw Billy Jack carry the football. Right then, I began to realize that, just like baseball had been, my days as a football player were numbered. I began shifting my focus from the game on the field to the game in the stands. I enjoyed playing football for the next several seasons, but I knew my potential was limited. The intricacies of baseball appealed to me, and I have been a fan ever since.

When Billy Jack took that first handoff and ran through the defense as if it weren't there, and then effortlessly rumbled into the end zone, I realized that there existed a level of talent that I had not yet been aware of. He was the most recruited high school athlete in a decade throughout the state of Oklahoma. He became a local legend when he signed a letter of intent to attend the University of Tulsa.

After four years of record-breaking statistics, Billy Jack was, indeed, drafted in the third round by the Dallas Cowboys. Nine seasons in the NFL left him bruised and battered but financially secure and living back in Tulsa. To say that he was a local legend would be understating the reality.

Then Billy Jack did a very stupid thing. Life had prepared him to handle a football, but not a lot of money. Billy Jack chose to invest virtually all of his NFL proceeds in an oil drilling company. His hopes, dreams, and life savings disappeared down a dry hole in western Oklahoma.

He sounded like an overworked halfback who fumbled and lost a double overtime playoff game the day he came to see me.

Chapter Four

As I carefully made my way down the hill from the Plaza building, crossed Riverside Drive, and entered Tulsa's River Park, I thought about the fact that I had never considered running as something in and of itself. I had obviously run to train for football and baseball as a youth—and the drill sergeant who had prepared me for my time in Vietnam seemed to think recruits should run everywhere—but now I was contemplating jogging as a stand-alone activity.

At the time, jogging seemed more like something designed to move me away from the dreaded middle age instead of how it had seemed in my youth as I ran toward the goal line or toward home plate.

Part of the long recovery process that had taken me from a newly blinded guy on the U.S. Army hospital ship, through many months of rehab, to the person I have become was mobility training. Walking with a white cane is an intricate skill that involves your sense of hearing, touch, and awareness of everything around you. There is nothing more terrifying in the beginning and nothing more natural once you master the challenge at hand.

As you improve with the white cane, you are able to walk faster, but I had never contemplated jogging or running since the time I had lost my sight. This is not to say that I would have contemplated it anyway, as most of my sighted contemporaries jointly approaching middle age were not running either. As I look back now, my sedentary life style was due more to my legs than my eyes.

During my first training session in the park, I decided I would walk a little before I began to jog. The asphalt path that runs through the park along the edge of the river is approximately six feet wide. Bicycles can pass one another comfortably while walkers and joggers can step off of the path to let the bicycle traffic go by.

There is an unwritten set of rules that govern walkers, joggers, and bicyclists in the park. Instantly, I realized that I didn't fit in, and the path was going to be a challenge for me, because it was not perfectly straight like the city sidewalks I was accustomed to; but, instead, the path meandered through the park, up and down gentle slopes, and back and forth following the course of the river.

The next problem I encountered was the fact that my ears could not always pick up the sounds of the other walkers and joggers as well as the oncoming bicycles because of the traffic noise from the nearby Riverside Drive.

This was exacerbated by what I call the Moses property of my white cane. When I was a youth in Sunday School at the Baptist Church, we were told that Moses parted the Red Sea by raising his walking staff into the air. Had it not been the Red Sea, but instead a crowd of people, Moses could have instantly parted them by merely displaying a white cane. Over the years as a pedestrian, I have noticed that walkers, joggers, bicyclists, and even buses will move over at the mere glimpse of my white cane.

On what I thought would be my first jogging day in the park, I found this phenomenon was holding true.

As I made my way along the path, conversations ceased, and people veered out of my way or stopped completely. This did not help me get my bearings as I could not follow anyone or determine the direction of the path ahead. As my frustration grew, I had to fight down the old feelings of panic that sometimes attack everyone that goes into a five-sense world with only four senses.

As I struggled along the path, I heard muttered statements. "Why doesn't he do whatever he's doing somewhere else?" "He's just in the way and doesn't belong here." And "Isn't there a special home or hospital for crippled people?"

There was a time when these words would have devastated me, but that had been a long time before. My immediate reaction was to push even harder and show them what a blind guy could do. While I knew this would be my eventual goal, I also knew that sometimes the shortest distance between two points involves stepping back, re-examining your route, and finding a better way to get where you're going.

When I finally heard the tapping of my cane echoing off of a bridge above me, I realized that I had gone less than a mile from my apartment and the familiar sidewalk of the 21st Street bridge was just over my head. I found the path that led up the embankment to the bridge and felt a sense of relief and normality as I began making my way along the sidewalk back to my familiar Plaza building.

There was a time in my recovery and rebirth when retreat meant defeat. But as I rode up the elevator to my apartment that day, retreat turned into resolve, and I knew I would overcome. Blindness has taught me that, although the conventional may not work, there is always a way for Jacob Dyer to get where he wants to go.

Before my first failed jogging excursion in the park, it had been little more than a lark or a whim. Now the prospect of jogging in the park seemed to be a matter of life and death.

Chapter Five

As the fading city sounds drifted through my office window, I recalled that fateful day with Billy Jack Johnson. Monica Stone, my assistant and so much more, burst into my office and intoned with that magical voice that only launched a thousand ships because more were not available, "Hey, boss. You'll never believe who's sitting out in the lobby."

I had rarely known Monica to be this excited. She is not generally plagued by hero worship like the rest of us mere mortals.

I asked, "How many guesses do I get?"

She replied excitedly, "It's Billy Jack Johnson, the Dallas Cowboys guy. He says he knows you."

I tried to appear nonchalant as I said, "We used to play together. He was pretty good."

Monica stated, not a bit sarcastically, "I know he's good. You're the one on trial here."

"Did he say what he wants, or is he just here to pay homage to my athletic prowess?"

She said, "He seems really depressed. I think he needs us, but I don't know how or why. I'm sure he'll tell you."

"Well, go get him and try to cheer him up on the way in."

She purred, "That will be a pleasure."

I knew that Billy Jack was in for a rare and unforgettable treat. In the cheering up department, or almost any other department, Monica is unparalleled, so I was quite shocked when a few minutes later, a totally dejected Billy Jack Johnson sat in the right client chair across the desk from me. I couldn't help but imagine the depth of despair that existed and was impervious to Monica's charms.

"Billy Jack, it is great to see you. How long has it been?"

He seemed distracted as he replied, "I guess it was the 20-year reunion. I didn't get to talk with you much then."

I tried to maintain my dignity as I replied, "Yeah, I remember everyone was clamoring for a piece of you."

Billy Jack began speaking as if nothing had gone before. "Jake, I am in trouble, and I don't know where else to turn. I don't know exactly what you do, but I've heard that you have ways to fix things that have gone wrong. That's what I need."

I paused and said, "Well, tell me about it."

He blew out about an acre of air and replied, "Jake, after I left the Cowboys, I couldn't find anything in life that worked for me. For several years, the endorsements came and I picked up a few jobs on radio and TV, but I never could talk that good. About a year ago, I couldn't believe it, but all of my money was running out, so I needed a great investment deal. I didn't know anything about it, but growing up here in Tulsa, I knew people made money in oil. Then I met the Reverend Clarence Hart. Have you ever heard of him?"

I chuckled and said, "Yeah, anybody who gets around has heard of the reverend. I think he is the founder of the Get-Rich-For-Jesus Club, but he seems to be the only one getting rich."

"Yeah, I found that out. I had seen him on cable like everyone else, but I never really watched it. Then someone told me he had an oil deal. I thought, *If you can't trust a preacher, who can you trust?*"

I couldn't help replying, "Maybe a snake, a politician, or an axe murderer. God has so many wonderful people on his team, like Billy Graham or Mother Teresa, but just one Clarence Hart out of a hundred great people seems to give everyone a bad name."

Billy Jack continued, "Well, I met him and he seemed really concerned about me running out of money, and he felt sure that I could get set for life in one of his oil deals. So I gave him almost everything I had left, and that was the last I ever saw of it."

I smiled as I sat back in my corner sanctuary high atop the Derrick Building. I remembered dealing with The Right Reverend Clarence Hart.

Here at Dyer Straits Lost and Found, we endeavor never to lie to anyone. However, over the years, certain individuals with whom we come in contact do, in fact, from time to time, get under the wrong impression. I have never felt an overwhelming responsibility to correct other people's false impressions. So, when I called Reverend Clarence Hart's office and told them I was interested in an investment, I got through immediately.

He was all sweet and nice until I told him the investment I was interested in had been made by Billy Jack Johnson. I let him know that I was calling on behalf of the Oklahoma Attorney General. I justified this in my own mind, because if I didn't resolve this problem, it would end up with the attorney general and as he is already overworked and would only put Clarence Hart in prison which would not get Billy Jack his money back, I felt that a slight fictionalization of reality was in order.

Apparently the Reverend Hart was practicing the oldest scam in the oil business which is to sell 10% of your oil well to 100 investors, therefore raising ten times the well's value before drilling a dry hole. None of the investors are ever aware of the other 99, so they lick their wounds and go away quietly in embarrassment.

I explained to the televangelist-turned-oil-baron that currently the only pending legal matter before me concerning him was that of Billy Jack Johnson; however, as Mr. Johnson was a high-profile local hero, it was important to the governor, and therefore to me as the attorney general, to clear this matter up without unfavorable publicity.

When I explained that his options were to return all the money he had taken from Billy Jack Johnson plus interest or spend the next three or four decades as a guest of the state, he seemed a bit wary, or even blatantly suspicious.

The reverend asked cautiously, "How do I know you're really the attorney general? Is there a number where I can call you back?"

I got indignant and threatened to withdraw my previous generous offer. He quoted some scripture about forgiveness, and I reluctantly gave him an Oklahoma City phone number that he could call back. I knew the phone would be answered by a talented young lady who was willing to masquerade as the operator at the attorney general's office in exchange for an upscale evening including champagne, dinner, and dancing. I am willing to make incredible sacrifices in the line of duty.

As arranged, my Oklahoma City dinner date received the call and forwarded it back to me. I answered the phone abruptly. "Reverend Hart, you have tried my patience more than enough. You have ten seconds to either accept my generous offer returning all the money to Mr. Johnson with interest or I will have the distinct pleasure and privilege of putting you in a maximum security penitentiary where you can preach your message to a group of very large, sexually-deprived, hostile people. Is there any part of this you don't understand?"

While not being a man of honor and integrity, Reverend Hart did prove to be an individual of clear and well-reasoned judgement. He agreed to make all financial reparations to Billy Jack Johnson within 30 days.

I knew that the first call on my answering machine signaled the fact that Billy Jack had just received the promised check in the mail. I was thinking, *Life is pretty good when you can help an old friend, earn an outrageous fee, and smash a disgusting bug all at the same time.*

I wondered what news awaited me as I pushed the code to hear my second message. If I had only known.

Chapter Six

During my next trip to the River Park, I was determined that things would be different. Originally, I had set out to do a little jogging and somehow forestall the ever-encroaching hands of time. While this may be a laudable and worthwhile pursuit, it is nothing compared to the challenge before me on that particular day.

I was committed to the prospect of accomplishing a task that other people thought to be beyond my abilities. I was determined to show them otherwise and, more importantly, once again prove to myself that, in a world divided by *can't* and *can*, Jacob Dyer still can.

As a blind person for these many years, I have learned that tasks that challenge normal people somehow don't bother me. It's the unforeseen details that can be my nemesis. For most out-of-shape, almost middle-aged guys, taking up a jogging regimen is enough of a test. I wasn't so worried about the normal concerns involving the jogging part. I just wanted to figure out a way to get to the park on my own and make it work for me.

In my life as a blind person, I've found that most of the difficulty in getting to the finish line involves finding and mastering the starting gate.

On my second effort into the park, I had determined that since there is an eleven o'clock curfew along the bike path, that I might find fewer obstructions just before the park closed; but as I entered the park at 10:30 that particular evening, there seemed to be even more bicyclists and pedestrians than before. Music was blaring from somewhere, people were shouting and rushing in all directions, and I was lost.

Realizing that my plan to arrive just before curfew was not working, I determined not to leave the park without another plan. In both my personal and professional life, I have discovered that even a bad plan is better than no plan at all.

As I struggled along the edge of the asphalt path, trying to avoid getting run over and not have a panic attack, my cane tapped some loose gravel at the edge of the asphalt, and I realized I had reached one of the park benches arranged throughout the area. The gravel is spread under the benches so that mud can be avoided after it rains.

As I took one step off of the path, my cane touched the edge of the bench. I felt the end of the surface and sat down quickly and tried to catch my breath and restore a sense of calm to myself.

As I sat there, I began to let my other senses work and take stock of my surroundings. It was a pleasant evening, my Braille watch told me it was 10:45, and the activity in the park that had been terrifying a few minutes before now seemed almost festive.

Mothers collected their children, bicycle riders bade one another farewell and scheduled their next ride, and I started feeling confident that I could master my surroundings.

Just then, someone shifted their weight and cleared their throat at the other end of the bench, and I realized I was not alone. My confidence in mastering my surroundings faded a bit as I turned in the direction of the noise and hesitantly said, "Good evening."

A shaky voice, somewhat out of breath replied, "Good evening."

Just when I was trying to think of another conversation starter that would get me some more details about my bench companion, a group of runners approached along the path. From their stride and pace, I realized these were not weekend warriors but well-trained athletes.

They stopped in front of the bench and one of them stated in a commanding voice, "I've been telling you for a long time you couldn't cut it, and you should voluntarily get off of the team. Tonight proves I'm right, and it's no longer your choice. The Tulsa Running Team doesn't need a broken down old has-been like you."

The others gathered around the speaker, laughed, and clapped. At some signal I could not perceive, they strode away and rapidly faded into the distance with their athletic stride.

I could almost feel the shame and discomfort from my bench companion. I tried to break the ice again, stating, "My name's Jacob Dyer, and it looks like either you or me is off the team. We blind guys sometimes get a little confused about where a conversation like that might be directed."

I heard a deep sigh, and then the voice from the other end of the bench said, "Well, Jacob Dyer, my name is Leonard Ryan, and I don't know about you, but it looks like I'm officially off of the Tulsa Running Team."

Leonard went on to tell me that he had founded the team 30 years before after a successful college cross-country career and nearly qualifying for the Olympics. Over the past three decades, he had made the running team and the competitive running scene in the Tulsa area the envy of the southwest. Some of the best 10K and 15K runs in the country, he informed me, were held right here in Tulsa, and most of them had been his brainchild and a result of his hard work.

The annual marathon in Tulsa had gained recognition nationally and internationally, and it had kept his passion for running alive.

"Well, Leonard Ryan," I said, "it can't all end like this. There's got to be a better way."

Leonard shot back, "You don't understand, and you don't know what you're talking about."

I laughed out loud and said, "You're absolutely right, but that never seems to bother me. I'm not sure what we ought to do, but if you will meet me here tomorrow night on this bench at the same time, we will begin figuring out a solution to both of our problems."

I didn't know it then, but that was the beginning of the race of my life.

Chapter Seven

Have you ever encountered a familiar person in an unfamiliar circumstance? I remember being eight years old and running into my third grade teacher in the shopping mall. I was in shock, because I had no idea she existed outside of my classroom.

The voice I heard on the second message on my answering machine was totally familiar but somehow not quite right. It took me a moment to register the fact that I was hearing the voice of Monica, but not her normal over-the-rainbow voice but a voice of despair, confusion, and panic.

"Jake, it's me. I'm phoning during the baseball game because I really don't want to talk to you. I just wanted to leave you a message. I'm going to have to leave town in order to deal with a personal crisis situation. I don't know how long I'll be gone or even if I will be back. I will let you know what I can later. I know you will be worried, but please understand this is something I got myself into, and I'm going to have to get myself out of alone."

There was a long pause during which I realized I was holding my breath. I thought the message had ended when I heard the small, distant voice one more time.

"Jake, I love you."

The connection was broken and, although I played that message back numerous times, I simply couldn't read anything more between the lines. The only thing I knew for sure was that if Monica had a problem, the option of staying out of it did not exist for me.

For as long as I could remember, Monica had been the spark in my life both personally and professionally. She functioned as my anchor, my eyes, and so much more. I knew that if Monica was gone, I had nothing to lose because I would already have lost it all.

Although Monica knew every detail of my life, including the terror and trauma I had suffered in Vietnam that had taken me from a carefree young man with the whole world ahead of him to this world of abject darkness, I knew very little about her. She came into my life, my business, and my soul at a time when all three would not have existed without her.

She was so much like an angel sent to me that her background and history did not seem important. Monica is one of those people who lives so much in the moment that the past does not exist.

I knew that she had come from a small town in rural Tennessee called Perkins. I knew that she'd had some bad experiences there that she didn't want to discuss or relive, so I had always avoided the sore spot.

After mentally sketching out a rough plan of action, I placed a call to the third member of our triumvirate. Franklin came into my life at almost the same time that Monica did. I had solved a potentially embarrassing problem for Mrs. Maude Henson. Maude is a relic from the golden age of the oil industry. She is heir to one of the largest fortunes in the world.

After performing the aforementioned task, Maude offered me the permanent use of her vintage Rolls Royce limousine and its driver, Franklin. The Rolls Royce limousine is priceless, and Franklin is better. Imagine Winston Churchill with even more bearing, dignity, and character, and you have Franklin.

He answered the phone on the third ring with a deep rumble that terminated in, "Good evening."

I said, "Franklin, this is Jake."

He sniffed briefly which signifies his commentary on things he finds self-evident, mundane, or beneath comment.

"I had assumed as much."

Cutting through to the heart of the matter, I stated bluntly, "Monica is in trouble. I think she will need our help, but she has asked us to stay out of it."

After a significant sniff, I heard him reply, "Obviously we will attend to the former and ignore the latter."

It took me several moments to fully capture his meaning, but I didn't let him know that.

I told Franklin that we would be making an extended trip to Perkins, Tennessee because I didn't know where else to start. I knew everything about Monica since she came into my life, so any trouble had to originate before she had come to Tulsa.

Franklin intoned, "Unless you have any special instructions, I will make all appropriate arrangements and be by to gather you forthwith. I should think within the hour."

As I hung up with Franklin, I knew he was as worried as I. The three of us share a complex web of interpersonal relationships that are as hard to understand as they are precious. I knew that he could not allow himself to show any emotion. He feels that his impenetrable façade is his own offering of honor and respect. He would not let it crack even though, in his own way, I know Monica is as special to him as she is to me.

Forty-eight minutes later, the doorbell at my apartment rang and, as I opened the door, I heard Franklin's familiar and comforting rumble.

"Good evening, sir."

Franklin's displays of emotion are limited to the previously mentioned sniff of disdain and the rumble, signifying pleasure or approval. It is nice to deal with a person whose entire emotional range is limited to black and white.

After another brief rumble, I heard, "Sir, I have taken the liberty of making all necessary preparations. Perkins, Tennessee is approximately a nine-hour drive if one chooses to obey all traffic laws. That notwithstanding, we could arrive in Perkins as soon as five-and-a-half hours if you deem it necessary."

I thought for a minute and told him that nine hours would be sufficient. Since Monica had requested us to stay out of it, we needed to be somewhat covert. One of Her Majesty's subjects such as Franklin, along with a vintage Rolls Royce limousine, and a blind man would be hard to hide in a town as small as I anticipated Perkins to be. I didn't have a clue where to begin, but I knew I would have nine hours to come up with a plan. That is more time than my profession generally allows.

Downstairs, Franklin opened the back door of the Rolls. As always, he gave me his brief rundown.

"Sir, not knowing precisely what to anticipate, I have taken the liberty of stocking hot coffee, champagne on ice, as well as your Sam Adams beer. Several appropriate hand-rolled tobacco products can be found in the humidor and, at present, Paganini's caprices are playing on the stereo unit. Your favorite movie, *The Ultimate Gift*, is in the DVD player, and I have already set it to play the narration track for you."

The special sound track created by the Narrative Television Network makes it possible for blind people to enjoy movies and television.

Franklin rumbled and inquired, "Will you require anything else prior to our departure?"

I told him everything seemed perfect. I settled into the back seat and heard the reassuring thunk of the Rolls Royce's back door. As the limousine floated across eastern Oklahoma into Arkansas in the middle of the night, I had everything I needed but a plan of action and a place to begin.

Chapter Eight

As I approached the park bench the night after I had met Leonard Ryan, I was hurrying along the path as I wanted to get there early and be settled if and when he arrived; but when I was still a few yards away, I heard the voice of Leonard Ryan say, "I wasn't sure you'd really come. In fact, I didn't think *I'd* really come. I couldn't imagine how a blind guy could help me find a solution to my problem."

I laughed and said, "A lot of people feel that way at first."

We sat, and Leonard asked, "Before we get too deep into my troubles, what are you doing here?"

I sighed and responded, "Well, it began when being an almost middle-aged, out of shape guy, I thought I could begin jogging or running a bit to regain my former athletic glory."

"What do you mean it began that way?" Leonard asked.

I took a deep breath and explained. "I have been blind for a long time, and I find that I am able to function in the real world when I force myself to do all I can do and most things I can't do; so what started out as a simple jog in the park has turned into a quest for me to figure out a way to master this jogging path and find my way back into shape."

Leonard Ryan just waited, so I continued. "I guess I've got to overcome my fear of learning how to run in the dark and find my way back home. I know if I can do that, the getting into shape thing will take care of itself."

Leonard Ryan proved to be a man of few words when he said, "It makes sense to me."

I changed the subject. "Why don't you tell me about Mr. Sunshine who kicked you off the team yesterday and what lead up to that point?"

Leonard paused and then began. "Well, the Tulsa Running Team always has eight people. They are ranked one through eight, and they compete in local and regional events. When I founded the team 30 years ago, I was the number one runner. Then, in my mid-30s, we had a guy join the team who was a real world-class athlete. I made him number one, and I slipped down to number two. Then, over the years, I have slowly slid down the rankings, and I've been holding onto the number eight position for several years. Dietrich Fulmer is the new number one ranked runner, and he's the guy you heard yesterday kick me off the team."

I thought for a minute and then asked, "Can he do that?"

"Well, yes," Leonard explained. "I've been hurt for a number of months, so I haven't been able to keep up with the team. And even before that, I was slipping pretty bad. These guys weren't even born yet when I was training for the Olympics. When I'm in shape, I can keep up a pretty good pace over a long distance, but I have no kick at the end. All of the spring and strength in my legs is gone. No matter what pace I keep, the young guys can just run me down."

Without realizing it, Leonard Ryan and I were becoming lifelong friends. There are some people you meet who trigger things inside of you that make you understand that you share a common bond or similar life experiences with them. As Leonard told me about a tough childhood, a stellar athletic career, and the rest of his life, I realized his struggles and mine had given us similar foundations and had brought us both to this place, at this time, sitting on the same bench.

The time just slipped away, and before I knew it, my Braille watch told me it was approaching midnight. The park had emptied due to the 11:00 p.m. curfew, and Leonard and I found ourselves the sole occupants of a quiet, deserted park.

Finally, Leonard Ryan said in the commanding voice that probably served him well as the founder and original captain of the Tulsa Running Team, "Well, are you just gonna sit there, or are you gonna run?"

I took a deep breath and replied, "Well, to be honest, I've been a little intimidated by this path, and I've had a little trouble navigating without benefit of eyes."

Leonard leaped off the bench and began stretching as he said, "Eyes I've got. It's my legs that are in question."

Over the next few minutes, after several failed attempts, we worked out a system where we could run in tandem—each holding one end of my white cane. As we jogged along the path, I felt the strain of muscles long unused, and I struggled to keep my breathing even; but, at the same time, the old exhilaration of my body beginning to do what I told it to do as I vanquished another insurmountable obstacle propelled me forward.

I staggered to a stop and bent over, hands on knees, trying to catch my breath. Without even breathing hard, Leonard said, "You didn't even make it a half a mile."

I caught my breath and stated triumphantly for Leonard and any vanquished demons still lurking in the night: "I know it's a long way to the finish line, but Leonard Ryan, you and I just made it to the starting gate."

I knew that Leonard had no idea what he had done for me, and I wondered if there wasn't some way I could do something for him.

Chapter Nine

A myriad of thoughts drifted in and out of my mind as Paganini's violin caprices soared through the night. I sipped on Franklin's gourmet coffee and thought about how I would find out what was wrong with Monica and how to deal with it.

Sometime in the predawn hours, I heard Franklin's familiar rumble from the front of the vehicle. "Sir, we will be needing to stop shortly for petrol. Might I suggest, if you would like breakfast, that might be an opportune time."

I replied, "Just pull off at the next exit, and let's find the first thing."

My thoughts drifted back to Monica and all of the various possibilities that might be troubling her. I began hearing repeated and virtually unprecedented sniffs from the driver's compartment of the limousine.

I inquired, "Franklin, are we getting close to something?"

Another sniff emanated as he replied, "Sir, I regret to inform you that it appears we have arrived in a locale known as Toad Suck, Arkansas. It is a difficult image to overcome in one's mind."

I shot back, "It's no big deal, Franklin. What are our options for breakfast?"

"Sir, I fear that our only option seems to be an establishment simply known as Gas And Eat. The sign does, in fact, boast breakfast around the clock. I'm afraid we may be a bit overdressed, however."

Franklin piloted the Rolls Royce to a stop in front of the Gas And Eat, opened the rear door, and I followed him into the illustrious eatery.

As Franklin opened the creaking screen door, he commented, "Sir, it appears that the captain or maitre 'd may not be present at this moment. We may have to seat ourselves."

We did so, and eventually a young lady with a pronounced accent of the South greeted us.

"Welcome to Toad Suck. Sorry it's taking so long, but everybody's outside looking at that fancy car."

She brought us passable coffee and over Franklin's protesting sniff, I ordered us both the specialty of the house, known as The Truck Driver's Breakfast.

After our waitress left us, Franklin stated, "Sir, it may be advisable for me to check on the vehicle and to tend to our petrol needs while our meal is being prepared."

He returned shortly and informed me that the entire population of Toad Suck had turned out to look at the car. Franklin sniffed deeply and said, "Sir, they are convinced that you are an individual they call Robin Leach, and we are somehow connected with a television program. I did inquire as to the origins of the name Toad Suck, but I fear that accounts are sketchy at best."

Franklin and I finished our breakfast, which I found to be delightful in a truck stop sort of way, and I even detected a barely audible rumble from Franklin's side of the booth. It simply wouldn't do for someone of Franklin's background to express approval over the cuisine in an establishment known as Gas And Eat in Toad Suck, Arkansas.

I paid our bill and tipped our waitress what must have been an acceptable amount, judging from her reaction to the exchange. As we were leaving, Franklin held the screen door open for me, emitting a final sniff as we exited. The clamor and commotion from the vicinity of our car reminded me of a county fair.

A gentleman rushed up to Franklin and introduced himself as Bubba Joe Carlisle, announcing that he was the "chief feature writer for the *Toad Suck Weekly Review*." He interrupted Franklin's extended sniff with a string of rapid fire questions.

"Is that a Rolls Royce? Who owns it, and how much does it cost? And why are you here in Toad Suck?"

Franklin turned to me and spoke discreetly. "Sir, if you will allow me, I will attempt to take matters in hand, dispatch these individuals, and hasten our departure."

I gave him a quick nod, and Franklin turned to the chief feature writer for the *Toad Suck Weekly Review.* "My dear sir, I must state—at the risk of being forward—that I find your tone and manner highly impertinent."

Bubba Joe Carlisle responded cheerfully, "Well, thank you very much. And who are you?"

After a long pause and suitable sniff, the reply came. "Sir, my name is Franklin."

Bubba Joe shot back, "Well, nice to meet you, Frank. So, how much does this car cost?"

A measured response was forthcoming. "Sir, the name is Franklin, and the cost of this vehicle is in no way germane."

"No, I didn't think it was German, but it is some kind of foreign job, and you don't sound like you're from around here, either."

Franklin suggested that the reporter might wish to step back to avoid any potential injurious situations. I met the mayor of Toad Suck and posed with him for a few pictures in front of the Rolls Royce. I turned down an offer to speak at the Rotary Club and an offer to join the First Baptist Church of Toad Suck.

Finally, when the coast was clear, Franklin opened the back door of the car and ushered me into the rolling palace which is otherwise known as our Rolls Royce limousine. Franklin got into the driver's compartment and started the engine. As it thundered to life, I could hear Franklin lower the driver's side window.

With all the dignity befitting the situation, Franklin called out, "My dear madam, if you and your Instamatic camera do not take heed and step back, I shall not be responsible for any encounters you may have with the front grill of this automobile."

We moved forward quickly, so I assume Franklin's advice was, indeed, heeded.

Being a formally trained livery driver from the British school, Franklin specializes in many things, chief among them being discretion. When I wish to talk, he is a wonderful conversationalist; and, unlike most people, he knows more than he actually says. On the other hand, when I wish to be contemplative or simply listen to my music, he is appropriately silent.

As we rolled out of Toad Suck, the absurdity of the last hour, coupled with the building tension I felt over Monica, made me feel like talking.

As we pulled onto the highway, leaving the metropolis of Toad Suck, I said, "Well Franklin, it's always good to take in the local color. I'd hate for one of you chaps from across the pond to spend time with us and fail to experience the real America. I bet you don't have anything like that in England."

"Sir, I am pleased to report that in all of my travels in England, all of the British Isles, and, indeed, the remaining holdings of the British Empire, I have never experienced anything approaching either the people or the atmosphere of Toad Suck, Arkansas."

I laughed and responded, "Well, I'm sure they would be happy to hear that coming from you, Frank, and I think they probably got a good photo of you, so you'll likely be featured on the front page of the upcoming edition of the *Toad Suck Weekly Review*."

The violent sniff that emanated from the driver's compartment let me know that I was approaching dangerously close to the cliff's edge which looms above the abyss of Franklin's patience and tolerance. Showing remarkable discretion for that early hour of the morning, I decided it would be a good time to experience the remainder of Paganini's caprices and begin to make an attempt to formulate some type of plan.

Chapter Ten

With each of our nightly running excursions, Leonard Ryan and I were making a little more progress. The progress was, however, slow and painful; but it was offset in my mind by the freedom I felt being able to jog along the pathway holding onto my white cane.

Then there was the night that our run ended with us both ensconced in the backseat of a Tulsa Police Department patrol car. In my profession—being the world's only lost-and-found specialist—I've had a number of positive and less than positive encounters with Tulsa's finest, so the fact that we were being held in the backseat of a squad car didn't bother me.

On the other hand, Leonard Ryan's day job consists of selling stocks and bonds and managing money. I could sense he was far less comfortable than me in the situation.

The young officer was apparently responsible for patrolling the River Park after curfew until dawn. As it seemed he was about 12 years old—or so it felt to me—I realized the curfew watch was probably not the highest priority in the Tulsa Police Department.

His voice actually cracked as he introduced himself as Officer Armstrong. I mustered my most official magnanimous voice and said, "Officer Armstrong, I want you to know what a fine job you're doing here in the park. This is an important detail for the Tulsa Police Department, and I can see from your performance they have the right man for the job; however, if you will just get on your radio there and contact your watch commander, Captain Brent Stacy, I believe we can clear this matter up."

Officer Armstrong leaned over into the back seat. I assume he was making sure we were secured so we did not escape while he was making his radio call. Finally, I heard Officer Armstrong broadcast on his police radio asking for Captain Stacy to respond.

Brent Stacy has been a friend for many years, although we argue like brothers, but we both know we would go to the wall anytime for each other.

Brent's voice came over the radio, and I could tell from the tone he did not like being summoned by Officer Armstrong. The voice boomed out of the speaker.

"What is it, Armstrong?"

Officer Armstrong responded on the radio, using his official voice. "Captain Stacy, I have apprehended two suspects in the park."

An actual sigh could be heard over the radio as Captain Stacy responded, "Armstrong, exactly what are these suspects being suspected of doing?"

After an uncomfortable pause, Officer Armstrong cleared his throat, and his voice cracked again as he said, "Well, sir, they were in the park, and it's after curfew."

I spoke up from the back seat and said, "Officer Armstrong, if you will simply inform your captain that you have captured the one-and-only Jacob Dyer, I'm sure we can get some action on this matter."

Armstrong was reluctant, but when he mentioned my name on the radio, Captain Brent Stacy uttered a phrase that would violate the established rule of radio decorum in the Tulsa Police Department guidelines. He told Armstrong not to move, and it was only a few moments later when a distant siren could be heard approaching.

The siren faded away as the other police car pulled alongside, and I could hear the door open and close. Then I heard the voice of my old friend, Brent Stacy, with a sarcastic tone that I knew signaled we were in for a bit of harassment.

"Officer Armstrong, have you thoroughly searched and handcuffed these individuals?"

Armstrong sputtered, "Well, no sir... I didn't think... I think one of them's kinda blind, sir."

"Officer Armstrong," Stacy said, "that's a clever disguise often used by Jacob Dyer. He is a desperate and sinister character."

I laughed and said, "Good to see you, Brent. Did they run out of donuts at the coffee shop?"

I could hear Armstrong gasp, and Leonard squirm uncomfortably at my impertinence directed at the Captain.

Brent chuckled and said, "That's mighty bold talk for a desperate criminal in your position."

We got out of the back seat of the car. I introduced Brent to my new friend and running companion, Leonard Ryan.

Brent said, "Mr. Ryan, it's a pleasure to meet you. It's a little curious that the two of you are running together, because you, sir, appear fresh as a daisy while your questionable running partner appears sweat-soaked and bedraggled."

Leonard began to relax and get into the spirit of the thing, stating, "Well, captain, I think it would be safe to say that Jacob and I are not quite on the same level in our training."

Brent laughed and replied, "Jacob Dyer has long been in the habit of biting off more than he could chew, and this looks like just another example."

Officer Armstrong inquired, "Captain Stacy, do you want me to run 'em in and book 'em?"

The captain's replay came. "No, Armstrong, Mr. Ryan appears to be a respected individual, and he has a stellar record in both the running and business community. On the other hand, I believe if we will just leave Mr. Dyer, here, alone, he'll probably continue jogging and may actually give himself the death penalty."

We shook hands all around, and Brent and I promised to get together soon for a couple of beers or a fishing trip.

As Leonard and I walked away along the path, Captain Brent Stacy could be heard explaining in no uncertain terms to Officer Armstrong that, "Yes, son, we're supposed to keep everybody out of the park after curfew. What I'm telling you to do is observe that order while you're patrolling anywhere other than where Mr. Dyer and Mr. Ryan are trying to jog."

Chapter Eleven

Everyone who works, regardless of their occupation, has unproductive hours and days. Those who labor with their hands and their backs, at least have sweat or blisters to show for the effort. Those of us who work obscurely with our minds seldom have anything to show, whether we are productive or not.

As someone who is dedicated to finding that which others have lost or has been taken from them, I often labor to locate nothing more than a stray thread that I can pull on and hope that it is attached to another and another that eventually will lead me to a conclusion.

In order to formulate a plan, one must have at least a thread to start with. All I knew was that Monica was in trouble, and the trouble emanated from Perkins, Tennessee. I had to resign myself to waiting for our arrival before I could begin to formulate any strategy.

In my years of experience in what we have come to call the lost and found business, I try to observe three solid rules. One: Never work without getting paid. Two: Don't get personally involved. And three: Avoid situations involving dangerous or angry people.

As we approached the Mississippi River bridge that would take us out of Arkansas and into Tennessee, I realized that I had already violated rules one and two, and with Monica involved, I knew if the situation required it, we would violate rule three without hesitation.

All of us have that mental list of things that "If I ever get a chance, I would like to…"

I called out to Franklin, "When we reach the west end of the bridge across the Mississippi, pull over and let me out."

If it is possible to make a rumbling sound ending in a question mark, Franklin did it and then said, "Very good, sir."

He knew enough not to question the situation, but I could tell he was a bit curious and less than comfortable. The Rolls Royce gracefully drifted to a stop at the edge of the bridge as traffic raced past us, heading into Memphis. Franklin opened the door, and I got out and unfolded my collapsible white cane.

I stepped up onto the sidewalk next to the iron railing at the edge of the bridge and turned back to Franklin and shouted over the traffic noise, "Meet me on the other side of the bridge."

As a blind person, it's hard to gauge the distance, scope, or size of large objects. I know how big an apple is because I can hold it in my hand. I also know that the Mississippi River is wide, but it's hard to get a picture of it in your mind while speeding across a bridge in an automobile.

As I began walking, I enjoyed the cool breeze on my face coming off the river. The smells of fish and diesel fuel were unmistakable. There were the sounds of tugboats straining to pull their loads upriver, and the whistles from the various ships echoed across the water. Several of the gull-like birds that congregate around any shore—be it ocean or river—drifted close to me.

I blocked the traffic out of my mind as it rushed by my left side. Just as people who can see have the ability to take in a whole scene or to focus and even stare at one small object, blind people and, indeed, all of us, have the ability to focus our ears on certain sounds and tune out everything else.

I could feel the bridge shake and sway as the large trucks thundered past. Somewhere near the middle of the river, I stopped and leaned out over the rail. There's a sensation that comes from great heights or vast space that is unmistakable. The great void, or nothingness, becomes like a tangible, living thing. It can become awesome and frightening but, at the same time, familiar and comforting. It's like the second ride on the roller coaster.

I continued my journey across the river with my cane tapping out in front of me and began to get a feel for its vastness. I couldn't help but think of those pioneers who had floated across this river on log rafts or those brave souls who forded the river clinging to their horse's back.

Finally, the atmosphere changed, and the sounds diminished, and I could tell that I had arrived at the eastern shore of the river and the western edge of Tennessee. As predictable as sunrise following night, I heard an unmistakable rumble signaling that Franklin was, indeed, where he was supposed to be. Being able to count on certain things in life make the impossible conceivable and that which can be conceived doable.

Franklin sounded relieved as he said, "Good to have you back aboard, sir."

He would never embarrass either of us by expressing the slightest bit of hesitation, fear, or concern. It's just not done.

As Franklin navigated through the traffic of Memphis, I thought about how all of us carry around a mental scrapbook in our mind or maybe in our soul. This scrapbook contains images of people, places, things, and events that have impacted us significantly in our lives. The impact may be positive or negative, but the clarity and vividness of the image is often dependent upon the depth of the experience. People continue to live as long as they add to their scrapbooks. They begin to die when they cease adding new images and begin to let the images that have gone before fade into obscurity. As a blind person, I am doggedly committed to maintaining and building a healthy scrapbook of life.

I mentally removed walking across the Mississippi River from my list of things to do in my life. Then it occurred to me that I should add to my list that someday, Leonard Ryan and I would run together across that same bridge spanning the great river.

Franklin piloted the Rolls Royce toward the east, past the outskirts of Memphis and into the gently rolling farmland of Tennessee. I mentally browsed through my scrapbook, including images of old friends, my time in Vietnam, my early days in the lost and found business, and my walk across the Mississippi River bridge.

And then, as often happens, I mentally turned a page in my scrap book and began to experience the stored images in the bulky section devoted to Monica. She came into my life at a time of utter desperation and not only made it possible for me to do what I do, but she gave me the will to want to do it. I knew that whatever the situation she was facing, it must be dealt with so that she could come back to the life we all knew and loved. I'm not sure whether I was more motivated by the thought of rescuing her or by rescuing the vital part of myself that she represents.

Chapter Twelve

My white cane and I have a perpetual love/hate relationship. I continue to love the independence and freedom it brings me while I hate the need to have it. A white cane is a tool that takes considerable skill to master, but it is also a symbol of things that it has taken me many years to come to grips with and that I still struggle with from time to time.

As Leonard Ryan and I continued our late night jogging along the bicycle path in the River Park, it became apparent that as a link or connection between two runners, my white cane was less than ideal. This deficiency became even more pronounced as I slowly started to get into better shape, and our post-curfew runs lengthened a little more each night.

There is no accounting for or predicting when you are going to have a breakthrough idea that creates a quantum leap forward in your world.

One particular day, I was reclining in my desk chair in my corner office on the 14th floor of the Derrick Building, contemplating these deficiencies in my white cane as a link between Leonard and myself. As I often do when I am contemplating, I was sipping coffee and smoking one of my favorite cigars from Panama.

A casual observer might confuse my deep contemplation as simply loafing about, smoking a cigar, and drinking coffee. Such a casual observer would be sadly mistaken.

As my contemplations stretched out for almost an hour, I was aware of magnificent Monica in the outer office making a series of phone calls as she moved back and forth from her desk to her computer terminal to the filing cabinet. She was energetic, efficient, and magical, as usual.

As I thanked the Creator for the thousandth time for whatever it was that brought Monica into my life, I considered the fact that she could move about freely while still tethered to the telephone, as the phone cord would stretch and contract to make up the difference.

Then, all of a sudden, in mid-contemplation, the idea hit me that created a quantum leap for Leonard and me.

Monica finally got off the phone as she obviously felt it more important to conduct our business that paid our bills and served our clients than to listen to my quantum leap breakthrough idea.

When I heard her hang up the phone, I called out, "Monica! I just had a brilliant idea."

She inquired, "Jacob, do you ever have any other kind?"

But before I could fill her in on the specifics of my brilliant breakthrough idea, Monica said, "Jake, I've got to run these things to the overnight, finish that research downtown at the courthouse, and pick up our client at the airport, so you're going to have to tell me about the latest chapter in the continuing saga of your brilliance tomorrow."

I got involved with several phone calls and the routine of the day and, before I knew it, I was almost late for an evening appointment, followed by my jogging rendezvous with Leonard at the River Park.

That night, my brilliant brainstorm proved every bit as great as I could have imagined. Leonard and I were able to run, still in tandem, but we were no longer confined by my white cane which was static. Instead, we were tied together by a length of phone cord that enabled us to each find a comfortable pace and adjust to one another gradually as we ran. Eventually, I was able to sense the slightest shift in Leonard's pace or direction from the tension on the phone cord and adjust my speed and direction accordingly.

The next morning, as usual, I was up early and settled into my corner office long before daylight. I was waiting on my first blessed cup of extra-strength coffee to emerge from the space-aged, supercharged coffee maker while lighting my first cigar of the day.

I made a couple of calls to Europe on a matter we successfully resolved involving some poor judgments made by a second generation member of a prominent investment banking family. The fruit had fallen farther from the tree than anyone wanted to admit, but thanks to the brilliant performance of Dyer Straits Lost and Found, embarrassment was avoided, face was saved, and a huge fee was earned and paid.

I was feeling appropriately magnanimous when the bell on the front door rang and her majesty, Miss Monica, entered like a sunrise greeting a new day.

I was just about to fill her in on all of the recent happenings when she asked a question that interrupted my train of thought.

"What kind of idiotic moron cuts off a phone cord?"

I made my way to her outer office, and she explained to me that some subhuman creature had disabled her telephone. I muttered something about crazed, juvenile delinquent vandals on the loose and found something urgent to do in my office.

Monica replaced the phone cord with a spare she kept on hand for some unimaginable reason, and I hoped the whole matter would blow over. I was quite certain it was not yet the appropriate time to share with her the tremendous breakthrough Leonard and I had experienced, thanks to the minor sacrifice of her insignificant telephone cord.

Timing is everything, and I knew this wasn't the time.

Chapter Thirteen

Without the benefit of a global positioning device, road map, or even casual directions, Franklin navigated the Rolls Royce ever closer to Perkins, Tennessee. He had never, to my knowledge, even heard of Perkins, Tennessee before I informed him of Monica's fateful message, but somehow—in his inevitable way—he zeroed in on our destination like a homing pigeon.

The closer we came to the outskirts of Perkins, Tennessee, the more urgency I felt to have a plan of action ready for our arrival. Our little trio at Dyer Straits Lost and Found is made up of two people, Monica and Franklin, who seem to have unlimited skills and unimaginable resources—and me. My sole contribution to the proceedings is to observe things in a different way and from a different perspective, and continually come up with a plan.

I realized that if Monica was facing a crisis, it must originate or somehow be connected to Perkins. That was all we had to go on as we sped across Tennessee.

Growing up in Tulsa, Oklahoma gives one a unique perspective in that Tulsa's about as small a city as you can get and still have most of the things you will find in a major metropolitan area. We have an international airport, a symphony, ballet, Broadway shows, and world class museums. On the other hand, if you're standing in the middle of downtown Tulsa, within approximately 20 minutes, without breaking any posted speed limits, you can be in the middle of the country or in one of numerous small towns that surround Tulsa.

Life in a small town is different from life in a big city or in the suburbs. Small towns are more self-contained, like a high school. Everybody knows everybody, and there are hierarchies and rules that are innate to those who live there, and are a complete mystery to outsiders.

The communication network in one of these small towns looks much like a wagon wheel. Many parallel spokes that are all close to one another but a hub that is connected to everyone and everything.

I consulted my Braille watch and realized we would be arriving in Perkins, Tennessee in the middle of the afternoon. I thought about the hub of the wheel and all the spokes relating to past cases and small towns, and I said, "Franklin, when we get into Perkins, let's drive down whatever passes for a main street and look for a diner or coffee shop. Usually there's one main establishment somewhere in the middle of the town where we should be able to find a place to start."

Franklin rumbled in agreement, and then inquired, "Sir, about the Rolls Royce... It may be a bit out of place in Perkins, Tennessee. Should we consider renting or otherwise arranging for alternative transportation?"

I thought for a minute and responded, "Good thought, Franklin, but even if we came up with a rusted out and dented 20-year-old pickup truck, a blind guy and a gentleman representing the pride of the British Empire would stick out like a sore thumb anyway."

I heard a sniff of derision that I assumed was aimed at the aforementioned pickup truck.

The Rolls Royce slowed as we crossed two sets of railroad tracks, and I knew we had arrived.

There were a series of brief sniffs, audible from the driver's compartment of our Rolls Royce, followed by a low rumble.

"Sir, approaching on our left is an establishment known as The Coffee Cup Café. I feel it fits your description quite admirably."

Franklin parked the Rolls in one of the angled parking spaces, almost perpendicular to the main street. Parallel parking is a skill reserved for those in big cities.

Franklin came around and opened my door, and we made our way into The Coffee Cup Café.

Franklin is a diligent and considerate traveling companion for me, but he does not put me at ease in the way Monica does. Neither Franklin nor I would ever feel comfortable holding hands so he could guide me, and he would never assume I need help any more than I would deign to ask for it. Over the years, we have fallen into a pattern of me following Franklin at about a 45 degree angle behind him as he keeps up a running commentary, describing our surroundings and any obstacles I need to know about.

We successfully negotiated the curb, the sidewalk, and the single step up into The Coffee Cup Café. Franklin described two rows of booths and a counter with stools running along one wall. He let me know there were only two parties seated in booths and no one at the counter.

I nodded and gestured toward the counter, and Franklin led the way.

Franklin and I sat on adjacent stools at the counter, and he both sniffed and rumbled as he informed me that The Coffee Cup Café was somewhere between the Gas and Eat in Toad Suck, Arkansas and my favorite restaurant in Tulsa, The Duck Club.

Squeaky shoes and smacking chewing gum signaled the approach of our waitress who informed us her name was Stella, and the pie was fresh. Franklin and I each ordered a piece of rhubarb pie, which proved to be, indeed, fresh, and exceeded expectations.

As another waitress seemed to be taking care of the two parties that were lingering in the booths after what must have been the lunch rush, I signaled Stella over, and she questioned, "Something else, boys?"

I am a great patriot and believe that the United States of America is the most wonderful country the world has ever known. Stella, the counter waitress at The Coffee Cup Café in Perkins, Tennessee, obviously agrees with me, because when I placed a hundred dollar bill on the counter in front of her, the mere glimpse of Benjamin Franklin stirred such patriotism and pride of country in her that she felt duty-bound to answer all of my questions.

Stella told us she had lived in Perkins her whole life, as had her parents and grandparents. She had graduated from Perkins High and had worked in The Coffee Cup Café ever since.

She stated with great pride, "I know everybody by name in Perkins and for miles around."

I knew we had found the hub of the proverbial wagon wheel, so I had great confidence when I said, "Tell us everything you know about Monica Stone."

I was flooded with despair when Stella stated with certainty, "I've never even heard of anyone named Monica Stone."

Chapter Fourteen

It must have been a slow news day, because the Midnight Runner headline and photo were prominent in that morning's *Tulsa World*, which is the main newspaper in town.

As I made my way from my apartment to the Derrick Building and rounded the final corner, Leroy Small—my longtime friend and newsstand proprietor—gave me his regular morning news and comment.

"Jake, all kinds of crooks, scoundrels, and questionable characters in the newspaper today, and lo and behold, you're on the front page."

Leroy stood there in his newsstand on the sidewalk and read the entire article to me, and described the accompanying photo in great detail.

He said, "Jake, you are looking good here on the newspaper's front page. You've trimmed down quite a bit, and your Charlie Brown *Good Grief* t-shirt is really stylish. It looks like you're working up a good sweat, and you're just about to go under the 21st Street bridge."

Then Leroy questioned, "Jacob, did you know you're tied to another guy with a phone cord?"

The article described in great detail Leonard Ryan's exploits as a world class runner and founder of the Tulsa Running Team and all of the surrounding activities in the competitive running circles. It mentioned me as a blinded Vietnam vet and referred to Dyer Straits Lost and Found by way of recounting several previous cases and exploits that had found their way into the *Tulsa World*.

Apparently, the extremely thorough and professional reporter from the newspaper had questioned Officer Armstrong about why people were running in the park after curfew. Officer Armstrong stated unequivocally,

"I patrol the entire length of the River Park constantly all night, and I can assure anyone that there are no unauthorized personnel in the park at any unauthorized time."

The article even mentioned Leonard Ryan's investment firm, so I hoped he might actually get a little business out of the deal.

Although I wasn't looking for any publicity, I had to admit that, all things considered, the Midnight Runner article was just about as good as one could expect.

I took a copy of the paper from Leroy and made my way into the Derrick Building and up to my 14th floor lair. I tossed the paper onto the sofa in Monica's outer office and dismissed it from my mind.

Sometimes, we all proverbially step into something very unpleasant and don't even realize it at the time. Later, we wonder how we could have possibly missed it, but at the time, it goes completely through our consciousness without registering at all.

I was in my corner office, oblivious to the building storm, and attending to some critical business details as well as the standings and box score with respect to the beloved Cardinals and trying to determine when the Paul McCartney tour might make its way to town, when Princess Monica made her daily entrance.

This always brightens up my day immeasurably, and I was basking in Monica's glow when she exclaimed, "So that's what happened to my telephone cord!"

I immediately realized the error of my ways and that I had totally missed the tempest headed my direction. I deftly shifted gears and inquired, "Monica, would you believe that I bought that phone cord at a street sale to benefit crazed, juvenile delinquent vandals?"

She huffed and puffed profusely as she stormed into my office and stated emphatically, "No, I wouldn't believe that for a minute. The only crazed vandal around here is you!"

This was when she made her tactical error and perched on the edge of my desk, at the specific spot where she sits when our conversations are ranging from professional and moving toward personal.

I thanked the creator for grace and mercy, and just smiled.

She said, "Well, are you going to tell me about this Midnight Runner thing or just sit there like a crazed vandal?"

Given those two options, I clearly felt that it was time to fill her in on my running exploits.

After I told her of my failed attempts to go it alone in the park, my meeting and subsequent teaming up with Leonard Ryan, and my near-incarceration by Officer Armstrong, I said, "Well, now you know everything I know."

She replied, "That's a sobering thought, but why didn't you tell me sooner?"

I sighed and leaned back in my chair, replying, "Well, I wasn't sure I was going to be able to do it, so I didn't want to tell you about it and then fail."

Monica soothed in the most reassuring voice imaginable, "Jake, if you had told me you had failed, it wouldn't have mattered to me."

I admitted candidly, "Yeah, but it would have mattered a whole lot to me."

Then she inquired, "So what are you going to do with this running thing of yours?"

I replied, "I'm not sure if I'm going to do anything with it. I just couldn't give up without trying."

Monica got excited and stated, "Well, now that you can do it, and with the newspaper article and everything, you need to pursue this further."

I paused and shrugged. Then Monica said in a voice that left no room for doubt, "Jacob Dyer, I didn't sacrifice a perfectly good phone cord and overlook your blatant vandalism for some passing fancy hobby of yours that's not going anywhere. I always expect great things from you, and I'm not going to stand by and watch you let me down now."

I gave the only reasonable response open to a relatively sane man. "Yes, ma'am."

I wasn't sure where the Midnight Runner was going, but I was sure he was going somewhere.

Chapter Fifteen

The silence hung all about us and reached out to the edge of the universe. I thought I had understood how much Monica meant to me, but at that moment, I realized I had vastly underestimated the value of my treasure.

Stella obviously sensed something was amiss and inquired, "Is this Monica Stone someone important to you?"

I was unable to collect my thoughts, much less speak, so Franklin took the ball and ran with it, answering, "Stella, my dear young woman, the aforementioned Miss Stone is, indeed, a person of great importance whom we must find posthaste."

Stella giggled and said, "You don't talk like anyone from around here, and like I said I graduated from Perkins High, but I'm going to have to guess *posthaste* means right now."

A moderate rumble preceded Franklin's response. "Quite accurate, my dear."

I stood up to leave, and Franklin preceded me toward the door in the long-established system by which I could follow.

Stella called out, "Good luck, and what about the hundred?"

I simply waved as we exited.

Next, I found myself seated in the back of the Rolls Royce, uncertain of our next move. I had a car, a driver, and a person I was desperate to find but absolutely nowhere to go that made any sense to me.

As I sat there, I reviewed all of the mental files of information I had and pondered each of my options. My old Vietnam buddy and eventual business partner, John Ivers, was fond of saying: "*If you're ever lost and you're not sure what to do, go back to the last thing you did that worked.*"

I began thinking about this little town of Perkins, Tennessee, which was the only clue I had to Monica's past. Next, I considered the aforementioned small town network and the proverbial hub of the wagon wheel. I clapped my hands and shouted aloud, "Franklin! A wagon has four wheels!"

This cryptic shouted comment was greeted with the rare and unusual simultaneous rumble and sniff. Had I not been so desperate to find Monica and confront whatever crisis that had driven her away from my professional and personal life, I would have noted the time and place of Franklin's simultaneous rumble and sniff to be accurately recorded for posterity and the historical record.

Eventually, Franklin inquired, "Sir, does the fact that a wagon has four wheels indicate that I should be driving us somewhere at this particular point in time?"

"Yes," I replied. "We need to find the First Baptist Church of Perkins, Tennessee."

Franklin obviously felt a sense of normality had returned as he had been given clear directions on how to proceed and a destination.

He responded, "Yes, sir. Upon entering this township and as we were motoring toward The Coffee Cup Café, if memory serves, we passed a large columned edifice that I believe sported a sign identifying it as the First Baptist Church."

Sometimes even a wild goose chase is preferable to admitting that you have nowhere to go.

It took only a few moments for Franklin to pilot us to the front of the church, and we made our way up the stairs and into the lobby of the church. It was obviously a solid and well-built building of massive proportions. The silence was all about us as the street noise had been totally eliminated by the giant wooden doors. If God wanted to talk to anybody in Perkins, Tennessee, his voice would certainly not get drowned out in the First Baptist Church.

As it was a weekday afternoon, there was no one about, so I told Franklin in a voice that seemed far too loud in the silent church, "We need to find the church office."

A reverent rumble could be heard, and Franklin directed, "A discreet sign indicates that we should move to the left."

A few moments later, I followed Franklin through a glass door into the church secretary's office. I commented to Franklin, "We have reached the hub of another wagon wheel."

A woman across the counter that I had been unaware of said, "I beg your pardon, sir? May I help you?"

I was a bit embarrassed, so replied, "Yes, ma'am, I do believe you can help us. I was just assisting my British friend here, to better understand his ongoing study of the westward migration in the United States utilizing covered wagons."

"That's interesting," she replied in a tone that assured both Franklin and me that she found it not the least bit interesting, so I continued.

"We are trying to locate a woman named Monica Stone and her family. Miss Stone grew up here in Perkins, Tennessee. We believe she has recently returned here, and we understand that she has a number of relatives here in the area. We were hoping you could direct us."

The church secretary immediately began rifling through a series of files, muttered several phrases that were unintelligible, and then proclaimed, "Yes, we had a family of Stones a number of years ago, but it seems they only came to services periodically and never got very involved with the church."

One could gather from her tone and demeanor that getting involved and attending services regularly was the very least one could do with respect to the First Baptist Church in Perkins, Tennessee. She wrote the address on a slip of paper, and Franklin and I headed toward the car with a sense of hope and direction we'd not had before.

Chapter Sixteen

When you begin any project in life, you start out by paying the price for success, but somewhere along the journey, you discover that you are enjoying the price of success.

Leonard and I were running along the river trail on a glorious evening. There is a certain pace that a runner can find that makes it seem like everything is in balance. You feel like you could, quite simply, run forever. Leonard and I had both found that pace, moving as two parts of the same organism, tethered by Monica's umbilical phone cord.

I was amazed as I calculated in my mind that we had probably already covered more than four miles.

We turned onto the pedestrian bridge which crosses the half-mile width of the Arkansas River south of downtown Tulsa. The pedestrian bridge was formerly a railroad bridge 75 years ago, and some rare and inspired public servant determined that it could be a wonderful pedestrian bridge, the crowning jewel of the River Park, and a Tulsa landmark. When the pedestrian bridge was completed, it became all of those things and more.

About halfway across the length of the bridge, there are several concrete porches or balconies that jut out over the river. We stopped, and Leonard and I walked out onto a balcony and leaned against the waist-high concrete wall that was the only barrier between us and the rapidly flowing river below. There was a fountain off to our right, and I knew that the lighted skyline of Tulsa was straight ahead. The traffic noise and activity in the park were a muted background.

If you could put sounds, smells, and textures into a postcard, this would, indeed, be a Kodak moment.

I was pleased to realize that I wasn't even breathing hard, and I had just run a four-mile stretch at a good pace and had fared almost as well as Leonard. We had become more than running partners. As my improving physical condition and prowess as a runner had developed, Leonard and I were able to have long talks as we ran. We were now friends.

I broke the silence. "Leonard, I want to thank you for all you have done for me over the past several months. I've gone from a hopeless specimen to a stellar runner in great shape."

Leonard laughed and replied, "You were, indeed, a hopeless specimen, but now you're closer to an adequate runner in good shape."

He paused briefly and then continued, "But, with my help and if you are persistent, you could become everything you think you already are."

Coming from someone with Leonard's background and experience, this meant a great deal to me.

I asked, "So, Leonard, what are you going to do with your running?"

I heard a deep sigh, followed by a recitation I knew had been rehearsed many times in his mind. "I used to be a great runner—maybe one of the best ever. Then I took a lot of pride in founding the Tulsa Running Team and starting all of the races and community running events throughout the area. For someone whose skills were declining, it was a way for me to keep active and stay involved with my passion.

"I always knew there would come a day when I could no longer run competitively at the highest level. I always told myself I would know the right time, and I would gracefully step aside and hang 'em up for good."

The silence extended between us, and I prompted him with a brief but probing question. "And then?"

He continued. "And then, I got shoved out by Dietrich Fulmer. This is a guy that couldn't have carried my running shoes in my prime, or even 10 years after. As the new captain of the team, it's his privilege to name the runners for the eight positions; but what hurts me is the fact that he replaced me with his little brother. Viktor Fulmer is nothing more than an arrogant little worm.

"If I hadn't been injured at the time, the other members of the team wouldn't have stood for him taking my place, but at my age, you don't bounce back and recover as quickly as you once did."

I asked, "What about now? You've been running pretty good with me over the last few months, and I'm quite sure I haven't been pushing the limits of your reservoir."

Leonard chuckled ironically and said, "I may have a little more inside of me than you've seen up to this point, and I know I could run head-to-head with Viktor over the long distance; but he would just kick into a sprint at the end and run away from me."

Leonard pounded his fist on the concrete wall in frustration and shouted out over the expanse of the river. "I don't care if it's time for me to quit, but I'm not going to let them shove me out!"

I let Leonard control his emotions a bit before I asked, "So what are you going to do?"

He replied resignedly, "Jacob, I just don't think I have any options left."

I heard myself exclaim, "Hmmmm."

Leonard asked, "What does that mean?"

I answered with more confidence than I felt, "Leonard, if I've learned one thing from looking for the light at the end of the tunnel while learning how to live in the dark, it is quite simply that we always have options."

Chapter Seventeen

Franklin navigated the Rolls Royce limo in a circuitous route that we later learned was the most direct way to get to the address the church secretary had given us. Franklin kept up a running dialogue alerting me that the neighborhood had gone from rundown to depressed to distressed and was approaching condemned.

Repeated sniffs emanated from the driver's compartment, and I knew things were not looking good from Franklin's perspective.

Finally, he stopped the car, turned to speak to me, and said, "Sir, I fear this is about as close as we're going to get as all that is left is a number of ramshackle structures covered with tarpaper and corrugated tin. As one seems to run into the next, and there are no driveways, mailboxes, or house numbers, we're going to have to go on foot in order to make any progress."

I thought for a moment, and Franklin continued hesitantly. "And, sir, every person in evidence for the past several blocks has been African American. So if we're looking for Miss Monica's people... well, our hound may be on the scent of the wrong fox."

When you live your life in the dark as I do, there are a number of things that don't make sense conceptually. Sighted people aren't forced to think of these things, so they never contemplate how absurd matters might appear.

For example, I realize—intellectually—that there are what all agree are white people and black people. Having spent half my life as a sighted person, I clearly remember that white people aren't really white, and black people aren't really black. For the most part, we are all various shades and hues of brown.

I have often heard people say, "Don't get white carpet, because it shows dirt."

Then with a straight face, the same people might say, "Don't buy a black car, because they show dirt."

No one has ever explained to me this incongruity between black and white. If all people were blind like me, the racial problem would disappear in about 10 seconds.

As Franklin and I emerged from the car and ventured out into this impoverished neighborhood, I realized that it wasn't as much a matter of black vs. white as it was a matter of green vs. not enough green.

Franklin spoke in a quiet tone reserved only for my ears. "Sir, I feel we're a bit conspicuous here. I'm not sure whether we're drawing more attention or possibly the Rolls Royce is becoming the main attraction."

When it was all said and done, Franklin and I were not forced to walk about through the entire neighborhood to find the Stone family, because the entire neighborhood came to us. Everyone was quiet and non-threatening, but in the next few moments, a gallery of people representing the population of the neighborhood encircled Franklin and me as well as the Rolls Royce limousine.

Finally, I assumed the gang was all here, so I cleared my throat and stepped up on the running board of the Rolls and announced, "Ladies and gentlemen and assorted young people, my name is Jacob Dyer, and this able gentleman with me is named Franklin. We are in search of a friend and colleague that has gone missing, and we fear may have encountered some difficulty. I am hoping that some of you here are the Stone family or can tell us where we might locate the Stone family."

There was an ominous silence, broken by a gentleman with a deep, gravelly voice. "If you found the Stone family, what do you want with them?"

I realized that life had not given these people a lot of reasons to develop a trusting nature.

I smiled in the direction of the deep voice and responded, "Sir, if I did locate the Stone family or if I am, indeed, addressing any of them now, I am looking for a special colleague and friend who grew up in this community named Monica Stone. We just want to help her with some trouble she may be having and take her back safely to her home and job in Tulsa, Oklahoma."

Another ominous silence descended when an elderly female voice rose from the middle of the crowd. "I am Miss Clarietta Stone, and all of my people come from around here, but there's no Monica Stone here or anywhere else that I ever heard of."

Miss Clarietta Stone continued. "Young man, my sister Virginia grew up blind and lived her whole life that way, so it took me a minute, but I recognize that look in your eye. So, I'll go ahead and tell you, all the Stones I ever knew were black like me; and if this Monica you're looking for is white like you, you're at least eight or 10 blocks too far this side of the tracks."

I was contemplating how to end this little one act play and somehow disperse this crowd when I heard a siren approaching, and the crowd all moved back but lingered in the near distance. The siren faded away as a patrol car ground to a stop a few feet from the front bumper of our Rolls Royce.

Both of the front doors of the car opened, and I heard a commanding voice say, "Nobody make any sudden moves!"

I assured whatever law enforcement official I might be confronting that no sudden moves were going to be made or even contemplated by me or my colleague until he gave the word.

He spoke in a tone that made me think he was used to being respected. "My name is Sheriff Oliver Shaw. I handle all of the law enforcement matters in Perkins and the entire county surrounding; and I'd like to know what you gentlemen are doing here."

I cleared my throat and responded with what I hoped sounded like confidence, "Sir, we are looking for a friend of ours and colleague named Monica Stone."

Sheriff Shaw tapped the top of his squad car door several times as he contemplated, and spoke when he finally had reached a decision. "Boys, I think I'd like to hear a lot more about this thing and how you fit into it, but since it's getting dark, I think it might be best if you came into the station and we discussed it there."

Franklin inquired, "Sir, should we follow with our vehicle or ride in the official car?"

Sheriff Shaw chuckled and said, "I don't figure anybody that talks like you and drives a car like that is an immediate threat to the peace here in Perkins. If I had you leave your car here, it probably would be down to the frame before we got to the end of the block; and if I had one of my boys drive it to the station and they had an accident, I figure that car's worth more than our whole town."

Franklin opened my door, and I slid in. He started the Rolls Royce and slowly followed the squad car back to the main street and over a few blocks to what he described as an olive drab cinderblock building with a hand painted sign proclaiming *Sheriff.*

Within a few moments, we were inside an overcrowded, overheated space with uncomfortable chairs. I may have had worse coffee in my life, but I couldn't remember where or when at the moment.

This was just the kind of place where I really hoped we weren't going to have to stay any longer than necessary.

Chapter Eighteen

I guess human beings can get comfortable and even casual about almost anything. I remember the first time I held a gun in basic training, and I literally shook all over and sweat poured off of me. Within a few weeks, I felt comfortable with both my rifle and my sidearm; and by the time I was brutally extracted from Vietnam via painful weeks on a hospital ship, I had actually reached a point where I panicked if I didn't have my weapons with me as they had become an integral part of my daily life and survival. I have heard of people handling snakes, swimming with sharks, and putting their heads in lions' mouths; however, there are unexpected moments when the snake, the shark, and the lion demonstrate their true nature, and we are all reminded that there are some things you should never take for granted.

Leonard and I were running farther and faster every night. He seemed pleased with my progress, and I was pleased that Leonard—through me—was staying connected to the running world he loved so much.

On one particular midnight jaunt, we had kept up a punishing pace for a distance beyond that which we had gone before. I became less aware of my surroundings and more conscious of my breathing, my heart beating, and the cadence of my arms and legs.

I could keep pace with Leonard automatically through the slightest tension felt through the now-familiar appendage—formerly a telephone cord. I was enjoying my new freedom, fitness, and independence when the snake struck, the shark attacked, and the lion suddenly slammed his jaws shut.

One stride seemed perfect and, in the next, my right leg went out from under me. I rolled over and over and down a bolder-strewn embankment.

I came to rest dazed, bloodied, and battered with my body laying half in and half out of the Arkansas River. I fought to maintain consciousness and to regain my bearings and perspective.

As a blind person, I need virtually 100% of my attention and mental faculties to function in the real world. I didn't know how badly I was hurt, but I instinctively realized I was far from functioning at 100%.

I began taking stock of my arms and legs to assess the damage, and I became aware of the fact that my phone cord was still attached to my arm, but it was hanging limp trailing away in the river's current.

Then I heard a voice, struggling for calm, but tinged with panic call down from above me.

"Jake? Where are you? Are you okay?"

I took a deep breath which generated pain from several spots and replied, "To answer your first question, I'm *here*, not that I could tell you where *here* is. And to address your second question, I'm not dead, but I fear that I'm far from okay."

Leonard made his way down the boulders and joined me at the river's edge. When he reached my side, he said, shakily, "Jake, I'm so sorry. I don't even know what happened."

I sighed and replied, "I think it was an attack of snakes, sharks, and lions."

"Oh, my God! I think you've got brain damage!" Leonard cried.

I chuckled and admitted, "Yeah, I was born with it, but I don't think I've got any more than usual."

Leonard and I both came to the realization that, among the many issues surrounding midnight runs in the park after curfew are the facts that it is pitch dark—more worrisome to Leonard than me—and there is no one around to help you.

Then I remembered some sage advice my grandfather had given me. "If you want anything done, plan on doing it yourself, and you will rarely be disappointed."

Eventually, Leonard got me settled on a relatively smooth and flat boulder a few feet above the river's edge. He beckoned me to "Stay right there, and I'm going for help."

I assured him I had every intention of staying right here.

I'm not sure how long I laid there, but I had time to think about where I had been, where I might be going, and how I had gotten here. I remembered that pivotal point in time, years before, standing on the middle rail of a swaying hospital ship in the South China Sea contemplating how easy it would be to just lean out over the edge and kiss it all goodbye.

There had been many heartaches, victories, tragedies, and triumphs from that point to this, but I got a new understanding—even lying injured and frightened on the boulder at the river's edge—that my life, such as it was, was well worth living and, more than that, it was pretty amazingly magic.

I heard two sets of footsteps rapidly approaching above me, and the ever-vigilant voice of Officer Armstrong. He called out, "Mr. Dyer, what are you doing down there?"

I wasn't sure how to answer a question like that, so I sought to eliminate the possibilities.

"Well, swimming is unhealthy, fishing is illegal, and sunbathing won't really be practical for another 12 hours, so to be honest with you, I'm not sure why I'm here, and I'd rather be almost anywhere else."

Officer Armstrong called down triumphantly, "Don't worry, I've got a flashlight!"

I actually was able to laugh and say, "It would be hard for me to describe how comforting that is to me."

An ambulance arrived shortly, and two highly-skilled emergency technicians strapped me to a board, slid me into an ambulance, and drove me toward a hospital. I realized that I had heard the sound of an emergency siren countless times, but it sounds different when you're inside the ambulance, scared and strapped to a board.

At that moment, you know for whom the siren sounds. And on that night, it sounded for me.

Chapter Nineteen

As the sheriff and two of his deputies sat silent and motionless, I told them what turned out to be most of my life story. I tried to keep it as mundane and mainstream as possible, but we went from losing my sight in Vietnam, through rehab, to eventually beginning Dyer Straits Lost and Found, to a point when Monica and Franklin joined the team, and finally, I described Monica's distress call on my answering machine during the Cardinals' game on opening day.

Sheriff Oliver Shaw let out a long breath and proclaimed, "I always figured if I did this job long enough, sooner or later I'd hear just about everything."

Showing that he was a seasoned law enforcement professional and skilled interrogator, he asked me a simple question that could serve to support the complex issues until he could fill in the blanks.

"How'd your game turn out?" he asked casually.

I rubbed my hands together triumphantly and exclaimed, "Cardinals, 6 to 5 on Albert Pujols's homerun."

"That Pujols is a heck of a ball player. I caught the game myself," the sheriff responded.

I sighed and said, "Sheriff, I'm really glad you knew the score."

"Son, you can be really glad that *you* knew the score," the sheriff intoned.

The sheriff leaned forward, shuffled some papers, and asked, "Is there anybody back in Tulsa, Oklahoma, that can vouch for this tale you've been telling us?"

I replied immediately, "Captain Brent Stacy with the Tulsa Police Department can probably tell you what you want to know."

He scribbled on a piece of paper. One of the deputies took the paper and left the room.

The sheriff inquired, "Can we get you boys any more coffee?"

Franklin was heard for the first time with nothing more than a derisive sniff.

The sheriff addressed him. "Sir, you don't talk much, but you're a good judge of coffee."

Franklin rumbled respectfully as we all awaited my verdict.

The deputy reentered, closed the door, and slid into his chair. Sheriff Oliver Shaw commanded, "Shoot."

The deputy began. "Got hold of Captain Stacy who is the watch commander at the Tulsa Police Department. He said Franklin here is an upstanding citizen with impeccable taste in everything but employers. He said Monica Stone is a gorgeous, talented woman whose only flaw is that, like Franklin here, she's not real particular who she spends time with. As for Jacob Dyer, the captain said he basically checks out, although he's been known recently to be caught up in some kind of underhanded activities after curfew in Tulsa's local parks.

"Stacy says that Jacob Dyer is pretty much okay, but if we wanted to lock him up here in Tennessee and keep him forever, it'd be fine with him."

I smiled and told the sheriff, "You've gotta love a dedicated public servant like that who'll go out on a limb to give you a glowing personal and professional reference."

The sheriff cleared his throat and muttered, "Don't push it too far, Dyer. I think after that glowing character reference, I'd rather see you on your way back to Tulsa than cluttering up the landscape here."

The mood in the office changed as suddenly as the temperature when an Oklahoma thunderstorm approaches in the springtime. Although we weren't all on the same team, at least we were all moving in the same direction.

I told the sheriff about my theory of small town communication networks and the wagon wheels. I filled him in on our trip to The Coffee Cup Café, the First Baptist Church, and the Stone neighborhood where he had found us.

He thought for a minute and said, "Son, your first three wheels didn't get you anywhere, and I know everyone around here myself, so it sounds like you got a full set of four wagon wheels, and you're still stuck in the ditch and not going anywhere."

The sheriff told us we were free to go. Franklin and I shook hands all around, and Sheriff Oliver Shaw walked with us out to the Rolls Royce.

Franklin opened the door, and the sheriff inquired, "You mind if I take a look inside this rig?"

We both slid into the back seat, and Shaw said, "I realize I'm just kind of a one-horse sheriff in a one-horse town, but I'm pretty good at what I do. And this town, such as it is, and these people, such as they are, matter to me. I'm pretty clear on the fact that you're on the level and this Monica Stone matters a lot to you. So I figure you'll be poking around town until something runs out that points to who you're looking for.

"The challenge we've got here is I want to help you without upsetting the electorate too much. So, I'd like you to keep me informed on where you're going and what you're doing."

I sighed with both relief and frustration, realizing I wasn't in jail, but I was back to the starting point; and I had to admit to the sheriff I didn't have a clue where I was going or what I was doing.

Chapter Twenty

Hospitals have always represented beginnings and endings for me in my life. I was born in the Tulsa Hospital where I now found myself being wheeled into an emergency room. My stint on a hospital ship as a part of my Uncle Sam's Vietnam summer vacation represented the end of my life as a carefree youth and my birth as the blind guy Jacob Dyer I have become. As they wheeled me along the corridor and put me in a cubicle in the emergency room, I wasn't sure whether this visit represented an ending or a beginning or something else.

They had not allowed Leonard Ryan to accompany me in the ambulance, so I found myself without a sighted companion as I lay waiting for something to happen or someone to show up in my emergency room cubicle.

Over the decades since I began learning how to live my life in the dark, I am never purposely alone other than in my apartment, at my office, or in a few other very controlled situations. When I first emerged as a blind person leaving the hospital ship and headed for rehab back in the States, my lifelong friend and comrade in arms, John Ivers, stayed by my side day and night. He was an ever-present part of my existence as I returned to Tulsa, and he was my partner when I opened what has become Dyer Straits Lost and Found.

Just as John was leaving Tulsa to move back to Texas in pursuit of his own dreams, Monica came into my world and has made all the difference. Then, with the addition to my ensemble of Franklin, Leonard Ryan, and a few others, I found that I had a perfect sighted companion for almost any situation.

But now, I was alone and felt hopeless and helpless to an extent that I almost had forgotten was possible.

Then I heard a voice that immediately helped me to feel calm and confident. I did not know if it was the desperation surrounding my current circumstance as it usually takes a lot more than just a random voice to affect me, but when I heard that Irish brogue tinged with humor and the wisdom of the world say, "So you be Jacob Dyer, the famous Midnight Runner I read about in the newspaper."

I found my voice and replied, "Yes, and who would you be?"

"Sister Mary Florene at your service."

I inquired in a less pleasant tone than I intended, "And just what services are you ready, willing, and able to provide?"

Her laugh put one in mind of springtime on the Emerald Isle. She said, "I specialize in all matters spiritual."

I groaned as I tried to move my legs into a more comfortable position and said, "I fear my current problems are a bit more physical than spiritual."

She said, "Most people think that, but they'd be wrong, and so are you. We have some wonderful people who will be joining us shortly to attend to your physical needs, and I will be right here to oversee everything else."

I wasn't exactly sure what she meant, but I had to admit to myself that it was a tremendous relief just to have her there.

Shortly, the squeaking rubber soles of a nurse's shoes alerted me that medical attention was on the way. The nurse informed me her name was Valerie, and she began poking and prodding to assess the most immediate and pressing damage I had inflicted on myself.

She said coolly, "That's a pretty nasty bump and gash on your head. Are you able to focus?"

I heard the disembodied Irish voice from the corner of the room say, "He's blind."

I heard a sharp intake of breath from Valerie, and she exclaimed, "I'll get the ophthalmologist that we have on call down here immediately!"

I chuckled, and she inquired, "Is there something funny about that?"

I explained, "My spiritual guide, the good sister here, is indeed correct in that I find myself lying here in your care and at your mercy as a totally blind individual; however, it may be pertinent for your chart that my blindness is a result of a head trauma experienced in the jungles of Vietnam and not on the bank of the Arkansas River here in Tulsa."

I heard the curtain across the front of the cubicle being abruptly opened, and someone with a long, confident stride entered.

"I'm Doctor Morrison. Why don't you tell me what happened."

I sighed and explained, "There I was, just your normal blind guy, jogging along the River Park path at a little after midnight, tied with a phone cord to a running partner and friend. Then, the next thing I know, I'm off the path, down the embankment, and half immersed in the river. And, before I know it, I'm being welcomed here by Sister Mary Florene, nurse Valerie, and yourself as an honored guest of this wonderful institution."

The doctor spoke as he began checking out my assorted injuries. "Either you have a weird sense of humor, or you've got brain damage."

"People tell me that all the time," I explained.

After a series of blood tests, x-rays, and an MRI, they wheeled me to a room and transferred me into bed. Dr. Morrison proclaimed, "We're going to keep you at least a day or two to wait for all the tests to get in and for a bit of observation."

The doctor strode from my room, and as the door hissed closed behind him, I heard a barely perceptible rustle of fabric in the corner.

I was just starting to experience the gripping fear that can come from not knowing where you are or who is around you when I heard the brogue of Sister Mary Florene declare, "Just your friendly neighborhood nun, seeing to your spiritual needs from here in the corner."

I discovered I had lost my Braille watch somewhere along the way, and the sister let me know it was approaching four in the morning, and my Braille watch was a bit worse for wear, having been smashed on the boulders along the riverbank.

I wanted her to stay but felt obligated to say, "I'm sure you have other duties to perform here."

Her laugh was like sunshine on the green hills of Ireland, and she said, "Oh, I haven't been on duty since just after midnight. I can't think of anywhere better to go or anything better to do."

I silently thanked her boss upstairs and drifted off to sleep.

Chapter Twenty One

Franklin and I sat in silence in the Rolls Royce parked in front of the sheriff's office in beautiful downtown Perkins, Tennessee. I had no idea what to do next and, eventually, Franklin took the bull by the horns, saying, "Sir, as it appears we will not be overnight guests of the local constabulary, and as nightfall is, indeed, approaching, I might suggest that we get settled in our accommodations for the evening."

I mumbled something about not having any idea as to what we should do or where we should go but was interrupted by a rumble and Franklin saying, "Sir, I took the liberty of inquiring with respect to the most suitable overnight accommodations for us and find that—while the options are limited—one establishment's recommendations extend head and shoulders above all others. Therefore, at the risk of overreaching my duties, I made tentative reservations for us to stay at the Trail's End Resort for tonight and a period of time in the future yet to be determined."

I laughed as I am continually shocked and awed by Franklin's courtesy and planning that borders on mental telepathy.

I said, "Proceed," and the Rolls Royce drifted along Main Street toward our new home away from home.

Several pleasant rumbles emanated from Franklin as we turned off the main road and began motoring along a crushed gravel drive.

Franklin described a beautiful old main residence surrounded by a number of individual cabins scattered throughout impeccable grounds that gently rolled down to a rapidly flowing stream.

As we got out of the Rolls Royce and I followed Franklin up the stairs of the property's original main house, I could hear the stream gently burbling in the distance. We entered a solidly-built room that served as the resort's lobby, and a pleasant, mature woman introduced herself as Mildred.

I stood behind Franklin and let him take care of all the arrangements with Mildred for us to stay in their premiere guest house at the end of the driveway.

Mildred told us, "It has two full bedrooms, each with a private bath, a wood-burning stone fireplace in the living room, and a fully-stocked kitchen. The back deck has a hot tub, and the best view of the stream below."

As she told Franklin and me about the history of the property, we learned it had been her family home for four generations, and she and her late husband had turned the property into a resort almost 30 years ago.

Just then, I had a brilliant idea. Actually, it was my only idea at the time, so compared to nothing, it seemed brilliant. I inquired, "Mildred, do you know a family named Stone and a young lady about my age, who looks a lot better and probably 10 or 15 years younger, named Monica Stone?"

She said, "Hmm," as she tapped her fingers on the counter and asked, "Can you describe her?"

Without hesitating, Franklin described Monica to a T. I could have done it myself; however, it would have confused the matter by creating the question: *How does the blind guy know what she looks like?*

When Franklin finished his accurate and glowing physical description of Monica, Mildred asked, "Any chance you got a photo? I'm a lot better with faces than names."

I was at a loss, as photos are not a regular part of my daily life.

Franklin rumbled and said, "Madam, here in my wallet, I happen to have a photo taken last New Year's Eve as Mr. Dyer and Miss Monica were emerging from the limousine at the New Year's gala."

Mildred muttered something about locating her glasses, slid the photo across the counter, and spoke as she peered at it.

"Thank you, sir. Obviously, that is you, professionally holding the door of the limousine; and Mr. Dyer, here, cleans up pretty well and cuts a dashing figure in a tuxedo. The young lady between the two of you is everything you described and more. And if I'm not mistaken, she is a young lady I knew years ago here in Perkins."

Mildred paused as I held my breath and time stood still. Finally, she continued. "It's impossible to be 100 per cent sure, 'cause I haven't seen her since she was a teenager, and you never see anyone that looks like her around here unless they're on a movie screen or something. But, gentlemen, if I had to make an educated guess, I would say that is Mona Stowe of Perkins, Tennessee, all grown up and sparkling."

As the silence stretched out in the lobby of the Trail's End Resort, I pondered and lamented the fact that the only constant I had in this whole situation was the fact that I knew who I was looking for. Now I wasn't even sure of that.

Chapter Twenty Two

A hospital has rhythms all of its own. There are regular and irregular activities that go on 'round the clock, day after day. They generally make no sense to the patient or casual observer. To the doctors, nurses, technicians, orderlies, and endless variety of personnel, it probably makes more sense as viewed from their individual perspectives, but I suspect if you viewed the entire process from a distance, it would appear to be a giant well-orchestrated organism designed to heal diseased and broken bodies.

I slept fitfully that first night—I suspect due, in part, to the pain medication as well as the strange sounds and smells of the environment.

I woke up disoriented on several occasions and could hear Sister Mary Florene in the corner reciting a strategic prayer I suspected to be at least as much for my ears as the Almighty's.

"Dear Lord, protect Jacob Dyer and be with all the nurses and orderlies tonight, here on the hospital floor, helping him to heal and restoring him to health."

I don't believe I ever got more than 45 minutes of uninterrupted sleep thanks to the parade of staff flowing in and out of my room, each on their own mysterious mission.

My favorite among all these late night intruders has still got to be the male nurse who actually woke me up to see if I needed a sleeping pill. When I confirmed with him that he had, indeed, awakened me from a sound sleep with his only motivation being the aforementioned sleeping pill, he failed to grasp the humor and irony of the situation.

Sister Mary Florene intercepted a number of these potential interruptions with a simple, "I'm here. He's fine. Come back later."

I'm certain she understood the importance, or lack thereof, of each person's goal in interrupting my sleep, so she could divert the insignificant and less important intrusions.

I have never really understood when day and night trade places. As a blind person, I suspect—in sighted people's minds—it has a lot to do with the arrival or departure of the sun, but it's not quite that simple. More people would probably agree on the criteria for when night has fallen, but the mystery of when a new day actually arrives is difficult to understand.

Most people would agree that two or three in the morning is actually very late night, and five or six in the morning is actually the earliest part of the new day, but that specific point when the transition instantly occurs is something I've been unable to pinpoint.

The hospital began waking up somewhere in the six a.m. hour and was fully awake by seven o'clock in the morning. The timing of the transition in the hospital probably has a lot to do with the changing of the shifts. At some point, the middle of the night intruder awakening tired people to offer a sleeping pill goes home to be replaced by a bright and cheery young lady bringing the breakfast tray.

I will not attempt to describe the full length and breadth of the deficiencies or inadequacies of the breakfast the hospital provided that morning. Suffice it to say, if one were not already feeling miserable, there was plenty in that breakfast to move one toward misery.

I felt weak, tired, and ached all over.

Sister Mary Florene greeted me with a cheery and angelic, "Good morning," that seemed miraculous coming from someone who had slept sitting upright all night.

As soon as the hospital rules permitted visitors, Leonard Ryan burst into my room and sounded as if he had slept less than me and felt worse than I did.

"Jacob, I am so sorry I let this happen to you. I just don't understand what went wrong."

Sister Mary Florene stood, yawned, and introduced herself to Leonard. When he started to explain to her that it was all his fault, she interrupted him, saying, "I've always believed that there's enough good in the worst of us, and enough bad in the best of us, that none of us should ever blame anyone for anything."

With that, she walked out of the room, and I heard the door hiss shut behind her.

Leonard sounded bewildered as he asked, "What did that mean, and who is she?"

I replied, "It means it's not your fault, and I'm still trying to figure out who she is."

Friends, relatives, and colleagues came in and out all day and into the evening. They brought flowers, balloons, and potted plants. I don't know who decided that these are the items that sick people need the most in order to get well, but I appreciated everyone's thoughtfulness and their efforts to provide tokens of kindness.

I believe a funeral would be the perfect time to experience all of your friends showing up and saying nice things about you, but since no one is available to attend their own funeral, the next best thing may be spending a few days in the hospital. The best treatment may be simply to be reminded that you have so many people who care about you.

When evening rolled around, there was another one of those subtle, unseen shifts in the day and night ratio. Visiting hours ended, prompting friends and family to drift out of the various hospital rooms and move down the corridors toward the elevators.

I was contemplating the prospect of being alone for the first time in this ordeal when the door hissed open and that angelic voice of Ireland purred, "Well, Jacob, me boy, how's the world treating you this evening?"

I said, "Well, I think I'm going to live to fight again another day."

She settled into her corner and said, "You're undoubtedly going to live.

I just want to make sure you leave here ready, willing, and able to fight another day."

As I heard myself say, "I don't have any idea what you're talking about," I knew that I did.

Chapter Twenty Three

As Franklin and I stood transfixed at the counter in the Trail's End Resort, our host, Mildred, did her best to fill us in on a teenager she had known of long ago named Mona Stowe. Her best efforts were sketchy and left us with more questions than answers.

I knew we would have to simply take this new piece of information and start over in the morning. Sometimes, it's just a matter of pulling on the new thread that has appeared and finding out what unravels.

Franklin and I settled into our cabin by the stream. Our accommodations exceeded my expectations. As the night chill settled into the valley surrounding the stream, we made good use of the hot tub on the deck and then enjoyed brandy and cigars by the fire.

I thanked Franklin for laying in provisions and thinking of all of the minute details. He puffed on his cigar and replied, "Sir, even when one must venture into the hinterland, there is absolutely no excuse for being without the most minimal creature comforts."

We talked late into the night about Monica and how little we knew and how much we would have to find out beginning tomorrow.

Eventually, Franklin and I made our way to our rooms. My last thoughts were of Monica and my understanding of the fact that I would have to do anything necessary to solve her problems, make the world right, and bring her back home where she made my life possible and complete.

I woke rested and refreshed. The standard panic of awakening in a strange environment never materialized, thanks to the pleasant chuckle of the stream flowing somewhere outside my bedroom window.

As I contemplated the day, the challenges before me, and the vast hole in my soul created when Monica left, I smelled the blessed aroma of coffee emanating from the kitchen area. I threw on my robe and burst from my bedroom like a heat-seeking missile, destined for caffeine.

I muttered, "Good morning, Franklin. You are a blessing. Hand me some of that coffee."

"Good morning to you. Here is some coffee, and you can tell Franklin he's a blessing when he gets out of the shower," Monica said.

"What...? How...? Where...?" I stammered.

Monica interrupted, "Jake, let's take it one question at a time. But first, Jake, why don't you swallow some coffee?"

I did as I was told, and as the warm brew of life slid down my throat, the world that somehow had been out of focus and off center clicked back into place. I knew that it had very little to do with the coffee and everything to do with Monica.

Before I could ask any more questions, Franklin emerged from his room. I know that, in his own way, Monica means as much to Franklin as she does to me, but while I was a blithering idiot unable to pose an intelligent question, Franklin greeted Monica's miraculous reappearance with a simple, "Good morning, Miss Monica, and good morning to you, sir."

Then I heard a rapid intake of breath from Franklin as he exclaimed, "Oh, my word, Miss Monica, what has happened to you? Did you run into something that bruised and cut your face?"

She sighed in resignation and intoned, "No, Franklin, I didn't run into something. Someone ran into me."

I said, much more sharply than I felt, "Monica, you've got some serious explaining to do."

She shot back with the same intensity, "So do you, Jacob Dyer. I left you a message and asked you to do one simple thing. All I asked was that you stay out of this. The next thing I know, you and Franklin are all over town talking to everyone. You guys and that Rolls Royce are about as inconspicuous as a killer whale in a wading pool."

All three of us stood silently and let the fear and tension we each had pent up in us slowly subside.

Monica rushed into my arms and gave me a hug, and the quiver in her voice let me know that the tears were just beginning to flow.

"Jake, I don't know how I can hate you for being here and love you for coming all at the same time. I really didn't want this whole mess to spill onto you and Franklin too, but I know deep down I wanted you to be here. The only sure way to get Jacob Dyer to come anywhere is to tell him to stay away."

I heard Franklin's deep rumble of agreement and knew I was outvoted.

Monica continued as she moved behind the counter and began preparing breakfast. "I am going to tell you both everything, but first we need some breakfast, and Jake, you're having a bad hair day and need a shave and shower. I think by the time you get all of that corrected and are worthy to be seen with Franklin and me, my gourmet breakfast should be done."

I have always done some of my best thinking in the shower, but that morning, I think all of my brain circuits were overloaded. There was one simple fact that I held onto. That was—whether Monica had found us or we had found her—we were all back together again, and I couldn't let anyone or anything change that.

Chapter Twenty Four

While your eyes may be the windows of your soul, they can also be a filter with a thick mesh screen or even heavy steel bars on them.

I remember, as a small boy, thinking thoughts and experiencing fears during the light of day that could never be spoken, but somehow, late at night lying in the grass in my back yard with my best friend Casey Fields, I could stare at the endless canopy of stars overhead and talk about the depths of my hopes, the wide expanse of my dreams, and the height of my fears. Somehow things that cannot possibly be spoken while looking at another person find voice in the dark.

That second night in the hospital, I was thankful to have Sister Mary Florene with me. Our conversation began casually as we discussed the extent of my injuries and when I could anticipate a full recovery. Then somewhere deep into the night, we connected and both shared innermost thoughts and secrets that had long lain buried for both of us.

She told me about being a young Irish girl, the fourth of seven children. Her father had been a sort of handyman who fixed and repaired things in their village and surrounding area. Her mother had been a cook in the home of a wealthy family. They had struggled mightily without complaint as the Irish have done since the beginning of time.

Her voice grew more fervent as she explained, "Then, Jacob, in my teenage years nothing seemed to fit. My older brothers and sisters were all finding their talents and gifts, while I didn't seem to have any.

"Then one day I stopped to see our parish priest to tell him of my plight. He was gone on a visitation, so I sat and talked with one of the nuns. Right there, in the church with the sun streaming in through the stained glass window, everything fell into place. I knew that I had come to the church to find the answer, and the church was my answer."

I asked, "Don't you miss having children, a husband, and... you know?"

She laughed and replied, "You never miss the things you've never had, and there's nothing better than knowing you're in the right place doing the right thing."

I told her about growing up in Tulsa and all about my carefree teenage years before that life ended for me in Vietnam. In the middle of the night as the hospital slept all around us, I shared the depth of despair that had washed over me when I had awakened as a blind person on the hospital ship.

I admitted, "There was a time I actually welcomed the prospect of killing myself. I stood on the ship's railing, perched somewhere over the South China Sea and was prepared to lean out over the rail and let all of my problems go to the bottom of the ocean with me."

She asked curiously, "So, what stopped you?"

I sighed heavily as I remembered that moment.

I explained, "My pilot and best friend, John Ivers, who saved my life by crash landing onto the deck of the hospital ship, limped out to that ship's rail in the middle of the night on his crutch and reminded me that we had promised we would either die here together or go home together.

"If you had known John Ivers, you would have believed—like I did— that if I had gone over the rail, he would have been right behind me."

I could hear the smile in her voice as she said, "Jacob Dyer, you must be a special man to have a friend like that."

I replied, "He was one of a kind. There'll never be anyone else in my life like John Ivers."

Sister Mary Florene laughed heartily and exclaimed, "Jacob, me boy, I saw that gorgeous young lady here in your hospital room all day, fretting over you and making sure the staff knew we had a very important person in our care. I saw the way she looks at you, and that is a look reserved for very special people."

I felt the warmth fill me that I always experience when I think of Monica's devotion to me, and wonder how she can feel that way about me when I don't always feel that way about myself.

I said, "Yes, Monica is a gift, and she is totally unique."

I heard that laughter again, and she said, "Wrong again, laddie. I spent some time today with that formal gentleman of yours. I believe Franklin was his name. Generally, those of us from Ireland don't feel too warmly toward those who are from England, but that Franklin is a special one. And Jacob, he would charge the gates of Hell with half a cup of lukewarm water for you."

I lay there for quite some time thinking about my life and the special people in it.

Sister Mary Florene declared, "Jacob Dyer, you will probably be leaving us tomorrow, and your injuries will all heal up in the next few weeks or months. The doctors and nurses have done a great job on your body, but I'm in the spirit business, and the important thing for you to remember is that whether someone's thinking about ending their life or living it any way other than the very best way it can be lived, it is pure selfishness. All of us have people around us who depend on us or count on us. If we're not there in every way we should be, their lives aren't the same."

I drifted off to sleep somewhere in the pre-dawn hours. I wasn't sure how I could meet Sister Mary Florene's challenge, but I knew I couldn't do anything less.

Chapter Twenty Five

Monica, Franklin, and I all independently realized that this was a unique situation and, therefore, we all silently agreed to waive our normal rule about discussing business at the table.

I was determined to remain calm and come to an understanding of the entire situation and then come up with a plan of action. So, as hard as it was to do, I sat patiently and waited.

Eventually, Monica cleared her throat and began. "Since neither of you obviously want to discuss the weather, the spring fashions, or even the Cardinals' baseball scores, I guess I'll start at the beginning."

A long silence was punctuated by her deep sigh as she spoke. "I was born here in Perkins, Tennessee. My mother was just barely 16, and I don't know how old my father was, because I don't know *who* my father was. The only parenting I had came from my grandmother, Lucinda Balfour, evermore known as Gram. She provided me with the best home and upbringing that she possibly could, but we were what they call plain white trash here in Tennessee.

"I worked hard and did well in school, even though deep down, I knew it probably wasn't going to take me anywhere. I was a plain, unattractive kid, partly because I didn't have the clothes, makeup, and hairdo that most of the girls had, and partly because I was a late bloomer.

"When I was 16, I met Cleve Grovner. He was a year older than me, and on the plain white trash scale, his family wasn't at the very bottom like we were, although as I look back now, they weren't much better off."

She paused, took a sip of coffee, collected herself, and continued. "Cleve was the first person outside of Gram to take a real interest in me, so when he asked me to marry him when I was barely 17, I thought it would probably be the best offer I would ever get.

"My grandmother had 80 acres and an old house where her parents and her grandparents had lived before her. When Cleve and I decided to get married, she wanted to give us 40 acres so we would have our own place. There's a ridge that runs through Gram's property, so she had the house down along the road, and Cleve and I got 40 acres up on top of the ridge. It's pretty country if you really stop and look at it, but I didn't do that very much back then.

"Since I wasn't 18 yet, the only way Gram could give us the property was to deed it over to Cleve since he was already 18. She also gave him a deed for her 40 acres and house with the only stipulation being that she could live in it as long as she wanted, but it would become ours when she passed away or decided to move out."

I could feel the tension building in the room as if we were walking down a long hall to open a locked door with something dangerous and frightening behind it.

Franklin's low rumble must have been reassuring, because Monica continued. "My marriage was okay for about a month and a half, and then Cleve Grovner thought the best thing to do was drink too much and beat me. Eventually, he lost his job, so I had to quit school and go to work hustling drinks in a local bar. I lied and told them I was 18. I remember thinking that whatever childhood I never had was over now.

"The beatings got worse, so eventually I moved out of the trailer on top of the ridge and moved back into the house below with Gram. Cleve kept coming around and threatening me. I was afraid he would eventually kill me or, worse yet, hurt Gram, so I left.

"I bounced around from place to place here in Tennessee, but just when I would get settled somewhere and think I was going to have a life, Cleve Grovner would show up to threaten me and beat me.

"After several years of this and one really bad beating, I got in my old car and headed west. The only thought in my mind was to get as far away from Perkins, Tennessee as I could. I ran out of money in Tulsa, Oklahoma.

"Later, I heard Cleve had gone to prison for manslaughter—something to do with a barroom fight—and I divorced him while he was in the penitentiary."

This sounded like a stranger telling a story about a distant time past in a foreign land. I was trying to make the images Monica was describing fit with everything I knew about her.

She continued. "I found myself wandering around in downtown Tulsa with two black eyes and bruises all over me. I was a mess. I took my last few coins and bought a newspaper. I sat down on the curb and started looking for any jobs I thought I might be able to do. I guess I couldn't find anything because, before I knew it, I was sitting there crying and the man I bought the paper from came over and introduced himself as Leroy Small.

"He asked me if he could help me, and I told him there was nothing he could do unless he knew somebody who wanted to hire a girl with no training and not much education that looks like she just lost a boxing match."

I could visualize Leroy and Monica sitting outside of the Derrick Building as she continued. "Leroy laughed that carefree laugh he has and told me he knew just the guy. He said there was a young gentleman right here in the Derrick Building who had started kind of a detective business with a buddy of his from Vietnam. They'd just been going a little while, and his buddy was moving back to Texas to work in some kind of family company."

I remembered the day John Ivers told me he was leaving the Dyer Straits Lost and Found business we had started together. John had gotten me through Vietnam, the hospital ship, rehab, and had helped me settle back here in Tulsa and get on my feet. When I knew he was leaving, it shook me to the core.

Monica gained some strength and said, "Leroy told me that what his friend here in the building, Jacob Dyer, really needed was someone that cared about him and would always do their best. Then he laughed and told me that Jacob Dyer was the kind of person that really didn't care what anybody looked like. So I screwed up what little courage I had left and walked in through your door. I was helpless, hopeless, and at the end of my rope."

I thought about that first day Monica had walked into my office and into my life. When she had introduced herself to me, we were somehow kindred spirits and the solution to each other's problems.

Chapter Twenty Six

The next morning, I woke up relatively refreshed for someone who had slept only a few hours in a hospital bed. The morning routine of the orthopedic wing droned on until Doctor Morrison finally appeared. He pronounced me well enough to leave and told me they wanted to run a few more tests, then the nurses would get my prescriptions ready and make arrangements for me to get checked out of the hospital.

The minute visiting hours began, Monica, Franklin, and Leonard Ryan burst into my room. They were all talking at once and simultaneously planning my departure and homecoming. Somewhere in the midst of the proceedings, Sister Mary Florene slipped out of my room and disappeared.

Eventually, all of the paperwork was apparently in order, and we were ready to depart. I was told even though I had spent a lot of effort and energy at the nurse's insistence to get out of bed and walk around the floor, I was now expected to leave the hospital in a wheelchair. Although I had great objections to this, there are some things simply not worth arguing about. So, as I got situated in the wheelchair, the nurse prepared to wheel me down to the elevator.

Just as she began to push the wheelchair, a violent sniff emanated from Franklin as he declared, "Madam, no one drives Mr. Dyer other than me."

Even though the nurse had the demeanor of a drill sergeant and the flexibility of a steel girder, she could tell she had more than met her match and allowed Franklin to pilot the wheelchair to the elevator and down to the hospital lobby where Monica waited with me while Franklin and Leonard went for the limo.

As Monica shuffled through the papers the nurse had given her, she exclaimed, "You would think, among all these prescriptions for painkillers and tranquilizers, they would have something for people that have to be around you all the time and put up with you."

I knew I must be well along the road to recovery since Monica's repartee was returning to normal.

Then, in a more serious tone, she said, "Jake, I'm glad you're okay, and it's going to be great to have you back where you belong. We were all really worried about you."

An uncomfortable silence fell between us. Then she said, "Well, here's Franklin with the limo. Leave the wheelchair here, because I don't want to be seen leaving with an invalid."

I felt a little shaky as I took Monica's arm, but we successfully navigated our way to the limo. I heard Leonard call out, "Hey, Jake. I have my own car, so I'll leave you here in these wonderful people's capable hands. I'll call you in the next few days."

I thanked Leonard and then, for the umpteenth time, assured him that it wasn't his fault and that I was looking forward to getting back on the road with him real soon. Even as I was saying it, I knew it wasn't going to be that easy.

As Monica was helping me into the back seat of the car, a shrill whistle could be distinctly heard in the distance. Franklin proclaimed, "Sir, the diminutive nun is rapidly approaching the vehicle from the opposite wing of the hospital. She is frantically waving her arms. Shall we pause here?"

Monica answered before I could. "Franklin, I don't know about you, but I'm waiting here, because her boss outranks ours any day."

Sister Mary Florene rushed to join us and said, "Jake, me boy, don't be forgettin' what we learned. I expect to hear great things from you in the near future."

Then Sister Mary Florene did something unexpected and virtually historic. She hugged Franklin.

She laughed and cautioned him, "My dear Franklin, let's not be forgetting there are more British Isles than either of us had thought."

Franklin rumbled in agreement, and Sister Mary Florene hugged Monica and said, "Young lady, I've given him some good advice I hope he will remember, but there's nothing better to remind a man he's a king than to go home with a queen. And my dear, you certainly fill the bill."

Without further adieu, the good Sister rushed back toward the hospital.

Franklin drove the limo even more steadily than usual, and it could barely be felt when we drifted to a stop in front of the Plaza Building. A few minutes later, I was comfortably settled into the familiar surroundings of my apartment.

Monica proclaimed, "There is absolutely nothing in all of this paperwork that indicates that the patient in question should not partake of a celebratory champagne toast upon arriving home."

Franklin rumbled jovially and popped the cork on a bottle of champagne that he and Monica had obviously set aside for this particular occasion. Monica handed me a glass of cold champagne and beckoned me to do the honors.

I pondered for a moment about what I could possibly say that could express the way I felt about these two people. Nothing came to mind, so I offered my normal salute. "To good times."

Monica echoed the other half of our toast. "And to the best people."

We clinked glasses and drank, and I relaxed, at least for the evening, realizing that while all of my demons had not been vanquished, they were at least safely locked away for now.

Monica, Franklin, and I enjoyed the champagne and one another. We talked of old times and good friends. We talked about our business and pending matters at the office. We, indeed, talked about the weather and even the Cardinals' winning streak. Eventually it became obvious to me, and I was certain it became obvious to them, that we were not talking about my past accident or the future of the Midnight Runner.

Chapter Twenty Seven

I was trying to rectify the vision of Monica as a young girl and teenager with the self-assured, competent, and magnificent person I have come to know and love. I was having trouble making both pictures fit into the image of the same person.

I can remember as a young boy getting into the attic in my parents' home and going through old black and white photos of my grandparents in their late teens and early 20s. The young, carefree people full of promise staring back at me from the faded photos didn't seem like they could be my grandparents, but I knew they couldn't be anyone else.

Monica had laid the groundwork of her past history, so as she continued, she brought us up to the moment.

"Then it was less than a week ago when Gram called to tell me what was going on. Apparently, Cleve Grovner got paroled after only five or six years in prison. He has been calling her and showing up at her house all hours of the day and night, threatening her. He told her the property is his once she leaves or dies, and he really doesn't care which one gets the job done."

Monica paused to control her breathing. I knew that tears of anger, frustration, and rage were not far away.

"Gram has heard shots from up on the ridge, and several of her cows have been killed, and the barn was burned to the ground last week."

Her voice quivered as the tears finally came. She said, "Then last Tuesday, she found her dog, Duke, dead on the porch. He had been shot through the head. She'd had that dog more than 15 years. Gram is my only parent, and there was a time when Duke was my only friend.

"Now Gram's afraid to even go out of the house, because she always hears shots from up on the ridge. You can see her whole place from Cleve's trailer, so Gram is a prisoner in her own home."

Monica paused and poured some more coffee for herself and then asked Franklin and me if we wanted another cup. We both said, "Yes," more to give her something to do than because we wanted more coffee.

She settled herself and continued. "Gram's been getting a lot of threatening legal papers. Cleve's brother, Walter, is a lowlife shyster lawyer, and he's making a lot of legal threats.

"I've been staying with Gram since I got here to try to keep her safe and to figure out what's going on. I went up on the ridge to see if I could reason with Cleve, and got this beating and more threats for my troubles. I thought I could confront him as a grown-up, self-assured woman, but he just laughed at me and made me feel like a scared little girl again.

"Cleve usually drinks all night and then passes out sometime before morning, so I felt fairly safe slipping out of Gram's house and coming here this morning. I hope he won't do anything to her if he thinks I'm there. I left my car in her driveway and caught a ride here."

I asked, "How did you find us?"

Monica laughed loudly and slapped the table, releasing much of the pent up fear, anger, and frustration we were all feeling and said, "There's only a handful of people in this part of Tennessee who don't know about the blind guy and the British limo driver in the Rolls Royce. Thankfully, I don't think anyone has connected you guys with me yet.

"They know you've been asking around town about someone named Monica Stone, but they know me here as Mona Stowe. Monica wasn't born until I walked into your office that first day in Tulsa."

I leaned back in my chair and thought for a minute and then asked, "If Cleve Grovner has lived up on the ridge above your grandmother all this time, why is he just now trying to force her off of the property?"

"I have no idea," Monica said forlornly. "I think if we knew that, we might know what to do. But Jake, I can't find out anything, and I've been afraid to leave Gram alone to go find out."

I suggested, "I think we should stay here this afternoon and until dark this evening and then sneak back into the house and get your grandmother. We don't want this Cleve Grovner to know you've been gone. I also think it would be best, for now, that no one around here knows that we are together."

I tried to put the puzzle pieces into place but didn't even have enough of the pieces to give me an idea of what the picture might be about.

Finally, I asked Franklin, "What are your thoughts?"

He rumbled and replied, "I agree that we should not divulge that Miss Monica has been coming and going from the house under cover of darkness. Furthermore, I concur that we should avoid the connection between us becoming known. I think we should ascertain what may have changed regarding the value or appeal of the property in question."

Franklin paused for an indignant sniff, then continued. "Then, sir, I feel we should confront these ruffians directly and be prepared to thrash them about if necessary."

I chuckled and replied, "Franklin, I agree wholeheartedly, and only wish I could have said it half as well as you."

A satisfied rumble was my only reply.

Monica expressed her concern. "Where will we take Gram? And I'm afraid to leave the house unoccupied."

I responded, "You and your grandmother will stay here, and Franklin and I will see that the house is occupied."

We all seemed to understand that we had accomplished all we could for the moment.

Monica slipped her hand into mine and said, "Jake, you probably want to take me for a walk along the stream and through the woods."

I did, and we did.

Chapter Twenty Eight

There is a connection between the human mind and the human body that I don't think any of us fully understands. The injuries from my midnight fall down the riverbank were healing about as rapidly as the doctor had told me to expect. I wasn't sure whether all of the pain I felt when I walked was in my mind or actually in my body.

We blind people have a tendency to get more than our share of bumps and bruises in the course of our normal daily routine. Table legs, corners of desks, and assorted area rugs can turn into near lethal weapons if they're not exactly where you expect them to be.

Finally, the fear and anxiety I felt about leaving my apartment was overcome by the sheer boredom of staying in it, so I determined to walk the eight blocks to my office in the Derrick Building and try to resume what has come to be known as normal for my life.

I felt a bit shaky and uncertain as I stepped off the elevator and walked through the lobby of my apartment building. As I moved outside onto the sidewalk, I began enjoying the smell of the fresh air and the feel of the sunshine, and before I knew it, I had forgotten all of my fear and anxiety.

As a former athlete and throughout my military training, as well as through my rehabilitation after the helicopter crash that left me blind, it has become apparent to me that our bodies perform about as well as we expect them to. Once we change our expectations, our bodies change the way they perform.

I remember, as a six year old, learning to ride a bicycle. The first few days, as my father tried to help me master the skill necessary to ride a bike, I became intimately acquainted with mailboxes, shrubbery, and the pavement of the sidewalks and streets in my neighborhood. Then there was that moment I can remember as if it happened yesterday when, all of a sudden, I became a bike rider.

I really don't know what changed other than, on one particular attempt when my father ran alongside of me holding the bicycle and then let go, I didn't fall over or run into anything. Over the next few hours, I became more steady on the bicycle, and I never again had any problems riding a bike. In fact, I'm quite certain I could ride a bicycle today if someone would simply steer for me. I have no physical evidence in my body to prove I could ride a bicycle other than my brain tells me I could do it, because I am a bicycle rider.

As I rounded the last corner and approached the entrance of the Derrick Building, I heard my friend, local sage, and purveyor of the news, Leroy Small, call out to me.

"There he is, the Midnight Runner, back from a near career-ending injury, ready to take up the torch and run again."

Leroy and I laughed and hugged one another, but as I went into the lobby of the Derrick Building, I knew my injuries were almost healed, but I was far from ready to take up the torch and run again.

As I opened the door to my office on the 14th floor, Monica made me forget all of my trials and tribulations as she greeted me and welcomed me back to work. I settled into my leather chair in my corner office and eased open the window to let the sounds and smells of the city into my office.

Monica went over all of the calls, emails, and correspondence with me and reviewed how she had handled everything in my absence. She was so competent and efficient, it made me wonder, once again, how important I really was in the Dyer Straits Lost and Found Agency.

Then, as our final task to get me caught up, she reviewed some personal calls that had come in which were mostly get well wishes from friends, and finally she got to the messages from Leonard Ryan.

"Jake, Leonard Ryan has called three times over the last week. First, he wanted to just see how you were doing and to tell you to get well. On his second call, he wanted to see when you were going to be coming back to work. And, finally, he called yesterday to let you know he was going to be running in the park and to see what you wanted to do."

So, there it was. What *did* I want to do?

I had avoided that question as long as I possibly could. I no longer had any physical excuse for not getting back to the park, so I had to admit to myself the lingering aches, pains, and scars were in my mind.

Then I remembered the nights in the hospital with Sister Mary Florene. She had known more about me than I had realized about myself. As the doctors were attending to my body, she was preparing my soul and spirit for this coming test.

I didn't feel much confidence in myself, but, somehow, I began to feel the confidence that Sister Mary Florene had felt in me. I was still afraid to try running again, but I suddenly realized I was more afraid of not trying to run again.

Chapter Twenty Nine

As Franklin cleared away the breakfast dishes and straightened the cabin, Monica and I walked out on the back deck and enjoyed the sensation of the rushing stream below us for several minutes. Then, hand-in-hand, we walked down the steps from the deck that led to a path that ran along the stream and into the woods.

There are certain times and places that are indelibly etched into the memory banks of our minds. We can pull them up into consciousness a month, a year, or a decade into the future, and they will seem as real and vivid as they were the day we experienced them. Maybe it was because Monica had been gone and now she was back, but that day—walking along the stream and through the woods holding her hand—will remain in my mental memory album forever.

We talked about everything and nothing, and then enjoyed the silence that is comfortable between two people as close as Monica and me.

We sat for a while, and she told me about all the magnificent sights around us. Being able to see is a precious gift that I enjoyed for the first part of my life. But having a loved one describe sights to you is a magnificent experience that very few people will ever enjoy.

We walked some more and eventually found ourselves at the main house which serves as the lobby of the Trail's End Resort. The owner and proprietor, Mildred, greeted us as we stepped inside.

"Hello, Mr. Dyer. I can see you found what you were looking for."

I leaned on the counter that separated me from Mildred and said, "Yes, I found her, and I want to thank you for helping me understand that my Monica Stone was your Mona Stowe."

Monica and Mildred exchanged casual pleasantries for a few moments as people will do who have lived in the same place but don't know each other very well. They talked about the growth of the town, friends that they had known in common, and all of the regional news including who married whom, babies born, and grandparents that passed on.

When their conversation was winding down, I interjected, "Mildred, we need a favor."

Mildred chuckled and said, "I bet you don't want anybody to know that Monica Stone is Mona Stowe or that she has any connection to you and the British gentleman in the Rolls Royce."

"How did you know?" I inquired.

She chuckled again and replied, "Mr. Dyer, I was born in the morning, but it wasn't this morning. And, if it has anything to do with those bruises on your young lady, you can count on me, and I hope whoever did that gets what they deserve."

My anger built as I replied, "Mildred, you can count on me that whoever did this will get everything they deserve."

We thanked Mildred and told her we were going to walk some more around her beautiful property. Just as we were exiting the lobby, Mildred called out.

"You may not be able to walk all the way to the upper end of the stream, because the highway patrol usually blocks it off when they bring the attorney general here for a little fly fishing."

I whirled around and asked, "Is Clifford Melville still the attorney general here in Tennessee?"

"Yes," Mildred replied. "How does an Okie know about our attorney general?"

I shrugged and said, "I just like to stay up with my current events."

Monica and I walked out of the lobby and headed toward the upper end of the stream.

Monica asked, as if she knew the answer, "Is there something about the attorney general that you want to tell me?"

"No," I replied. "I think it will all become apparent here in just a few moments.

We walked a few minutes along the path before Monica alerted me that there was, indeed, a Tennessee Highway Patrol car parked across the path with a trooper leaning on the hood. She described a lone fisherman wading in the stream a few dozen yards past the highway patrol car.

As we got within comfortable speaking distance of the highway patrolman, he said, "Good morning, folks. I see you're out for a stroll, enjoying the sights on this beautiful morning."

I nodded and replied much louder than necessary, "Yes, officer, it's nice to get out in nature and get away from slimy politicians and other lowlifes that inhabit our cities."

The highway patrolman acquired an official tone, sensing a potential threat.

"Just hold it right there and explain what you're talking about."

I continued, almost shouting, "I'M TALKING ABOUT WORTHLESS SUBHUMAN POLITICIANS LIKE CLIFFORD MELVILLE. THE KIND OF GUY WHO WILL CHEAT A BLIND MAN IN AN HONEST GAME OF DOMINOES."

Laughter thundered from the stream below, and I could hear the fisherman wading ashore.

He called, "Officer Wagner, you can't even get a little peace and quiet while you're trying to fish without some lunatic Vietnam vet harassing you."

Clifford Melville and I hugged one another and exchanged more insults. Then, finally, I introduced him to Monica, and the attorney general of the great state of Tennessee explained to Monica and the highway patrolman, "Ms. Stone and Officer Wagner, I met Jacob Dyer when I was recovering from a war wound in my shoulder on a hospital ship in the South China Sea off the coast of Vietnam. It's bad enough to be wounded in action defending your country and making the world safe for democracy, but when you have to endure weeks of pain and suffering in a hospital bed next to Jacob Dyer, it's inhuman."

Cliff and I talked of days gone by and our lives these many years later.

Finally, my old friend asked, "So, Jacob, what are you doing here in Tennessee? I thought Oklahoma had the pleasure and distinction of claiming you as a resident."

I briefly shared the events that had led up to Monica and me being in Tennessee. Clifford Melville took on an official tone that reminded me he was, indeed, Tennessee's attorney general.

"This sounds dangerous. What can I do to help?"

I thought for a minute and said, "I don't know yet."

As we parted, Clifford Melville hugged me again and said, "Jacob Dyer, don't forget who your friends are."

Chapter Thirty

It took me three days before I worked up the courage to call Leonard Ryan back. Somehow calling him represented confronting all of my fears and doubts. In one stumble and fall down the riverbank, I had lost all of my confidence, and it had been replaced with an unexplainable fear. Somehow, the very thought of running again morphed into all of my fearful memories of having our helicopter hit in Vietnam, the crash landing on the hospital ship, and my interminable struggle through the dark tunnel of rehab and recovery before I emerged into the light of day.

With my last shred of self-confidence, I dialed the seven digits of Leonard's office number. I heard his cheery voice on the other end.

"Hello, this is Leonard Ryan. How can I help you?"

After a few seconds, or maybe a few years, he tried again. "Hello?"

Just before he hung up, I croaked, "It's Jake."

Leonard responded, full of excitement, "Jake, it's good to hear from you. How have you been, and what are you doing?"

I explained that I had been getting better and taking care of business here at the office. When I inquired, he let me know he had been taking care of all the details on his job, and he explained, "I've been running a few times, but it's really not the same without you."

I thought of a million possible ways to try to change the subject, but none of them seemed even plausible, so I simply let the silence stretch out between us.

Finally, he tried again. "Jake, I think we should meet at our bench in the park."

I heard the anguish and guilt in his voice, and I knew he still blamed himself for my injuries. More for Leonard than myself, I responded, "Yeah, I would be up for meeting you in the park on our bench."

We agreed that 10:30 that night would be a good time to meet.

Before I hung up, I declared, "Leonard, please understand, I said I would meet you in the park on the bench, and that's what I'm going to do—meet you in the park and sit on the bench. I'm not talking about running."

After an uncomfortable silence, Leonard croaked, "I understand," and we hung up.

Often, dreading a thing is far worse than the thing itself. The great philosopher reminded us that a coward dies a thousand deaths and the brave soul but once. I had seen this on athletic fields as a youth and in Vietnam as a soldier. People who worried about getting hurt or killed suffered all of the time and seemed to be more prone to meet with a bad fate. Those carefree individuals who went about their daily routine expecting good outcomes, most often got one.

I was aware of this intellectually, but somehow, throughout the rest of the day, I could not project positive thoughts and expectations toward my return to the park. Monica sensed my tension and seemed to be aware of my pending ordeal. She kept me busy the rest of the afternoon and, just as we were winding down at the end of the workday, she declared, "Jacob Dyer, do you realize how long it's been since you took me out for a great dinner and celebratory evening?"

I chuckled and admitted I didn't know how long that had been, and further admitted I didn't realize we had anything to celebrate.

She said, "That's why you're so lucky to have me. If you can't remember our last celebratory dinner, it's been too long; and if you getting out of the hospital and recovering isn't cause for celebration, I don't know what is."

I couldn't think of an argument for that, and even if I could have, I would have kept it to myself as an evening with Monica is always something to be treasured.

We had a marvelous dinner at the Duck Club, including wonderful conversation and great wine. I offered one of my favorite Benjamin Franklin quotes as a toast. "Great wine is proof that God loves us and wants us to be happy."

Once again, Hamid proved that he is still the world's greatest waiter.

Finally, I had to ask Monica, "So, did you know that I was going to meet Leonard in the park later tonight?"

She reached out and put her hand over mine on the table and replied, "I didn't know for sure, but I thought when you asked for Leonard Ryan's office number that it would probably come up."

We didn't speak of it any more until Monica dropped me off at my apartment and left me with the statement, "Jacob Dyer, you can do anything you decide to do, and I will love you whatever you decide."

Monica's words echoed in my mind as I changed into my sweat suit and running shoes. The thought crossed my mind that I didn't need to wear my running gear to meet Leonard in the park and sit on the bench, but it's always good to be comfortable, and sometimes our subconscious or the powers that be that we don't understand know better than we do.

With fear and trepidation, I somehow navigated my way from my apartment into the River Park, crossed the bicycle and running trail, and sat on the bench. I was breathing heavy and covered in sweat. Any passerby would have assumed that I had finished a three mile run.

I had planned to get there early so I could calm myself before Leonard arrived. I realized, as far as running was concerned, I hadn't taken my first step, but I knew somehow just making it to the bench represented completing an Olympic marathon.

Chapter Thirty One

Monica and I found ourselves standing on the deck over the rushing stream at the conclusion of our morning walk. I think both of us wanted to prolong the moment, because we instinctively knew that once we went into the cabin, we would have to begin our work which included delving into all of the unpleasantness from Monica's past that was creating danger in the present and uncertainty in the future.

As we turned to go inside, Monica squeezed my hand and said, "Whatever happens, I want to thank you."

I answered, "Whatever happens, you're more than welcome."

In our absence, Franklin had cleared the breakfast dishes, straightened the cabin, and the pleasant aroma told me he had brewed a fresh pot of coffee. We sat down at the kitchen table and Franklin got the ball rolling.

"Sir, while you and Miss Monica were engaged in your morning constitutional, I took the liberty of preparing a relief map."

Anyone eavesdropping might have been perplexed, but in our little triumvirate, it was self-evident that the morning constitutional was the walk that Monica and I had taken, and a relief map was a wonderful device Franklin and Monica had engineered years before to give me perspective and a bird's-eye view of the vicinity.

Franklin had taken a standard folding map of the region and had flattened it out on the table. Then, using a combination of electrical tape and an Exacto knife blade, he had altered the map of the region around Perkins, Tennessee, so that I could become familiar with the area by touch.

Monica and Franklin sat silently as I became familiar with the area and burned the landmarks into my brain for future reference. I found the main highway we had traveled on from Memphis, represented by electrical tape, running along the bottom edge of the map. Then I found another highway angling from the top of the map and running diagonally from corner to corner, ending where it intersected with the first highway.

The two highways made a giant V sitting on its side, pointing to the right, or east, as I explored the map. Right in the middle of the opening of this V, near the left edge of the map, sat little Perkins, Tennessee.

Perkins was indicated by a number of indentations in the map's surface that Franklin had created with his knife blade. A number of smaller roads were similarly indicated. Several minor rivers, and even the stream our cabin was located on, were represented by a dotted line of tiny pinpricks.

Lucinda Balfour's 80 acres was shown by a rectangle of electrical tape located near the center of the relief map. As I touched the small piece of electrical tape that represented Monica's past and our current problems, I knew that the center of the current universe had to be there.

When I finally felt that I had a thorough understanding of the map and the general vicinity it represented, I asked Monica, "So why, after all these years, does your ex-husband Cleve, suddenly have an interest in this little piece of property?"

"I have no idea," Monica said. "It's basically a pretty useless piece of ground that's not worth much to anybody except our family. Gram lives on the lower 40 acres. It supports a few cows and, over the years, she has scratched a prize-winning garden out of the rocky soil.

"The property she gave to Cleve is up on top of a wooded ridge that's not good for much of anything other than the fact that it's really beautiful up there. From Cleve's trailer, he can watch everything that goes on in most of the valley and all of Gram's property."

Franklin inquired, "Miss Monica, could the value have increased unbeknownst to you while you have been living in Tulsa?"

Monica tapped her manicured fingernails on the edge of her coffee cup and considered for a moment. Finally, she answered, "Franklin, I just can't imagine why that property would be valuable to Cleve or anyone else other than Gram and me. She wanted me to have all of the property, but since I wasn't 18 yet, she had to deed the upper 40 acres to Cleve along with the option for the lower 40 acres.

"As I'm sure you can imagine, Cleve never got around to putting my name on the deed or the option, so if he can force Gram out of her house, he'll own everything."

I mused, "Everyone does everything that they do for a reason. Just because the reason is not obvious to us yet doesn't mean there isn't one."

Franklin rumbled in agreement and in approval.

Since we had all of the afternoon and early evening before darkness would allow us to travel to Monica's grandmother's property without being noticed, I declared, "It is time to split up and find out what we don't know."

I thought for a few minutes then stated, "There are only two loose threads we can start pulling on to see where they lead us. They are Cleve's brother Walter Grovner and any reason for the sudden interest in the property."

We determined that Franklin should go back into Perkins and, under the guise of doing some kind of genealogical research, he would find out all he could about Walter Grovner. Meanwhile, Monica and I would work the phone and the Internet to try and figure out what had changed in the value or desirability of that 40 acres.

I didn't have high hopes that our afternoon efforts would yield much, but anything would be more than we had.

Chapter Thirty Two

Leonard Ryan joined me on the park bench and broke the ice by simply saying, "Hi."

Not knowing what to say, I responded in kind. "Hi."

The uncomfortable silence was broken when both of us burst into laughter as we considered the absurdity of our situation.

I said, "I haven't been this uncomfortable sitting on a park bench since my first date."

Leonard laughed and said, "Well, if my first date had looked like you, I would have been uncomfortable too."

Then he asked awkwardly, "So, Jake, how do you feel?"

I blew out a whole arena full of air and said, "Physically, I feel pretty good although I'm a little weak and out of shape, but mentally, I'm really shot. I can't imagine running full speed along this path next to the river attached to nothing more than a phone cord."

Leonard stood and said, "If you don't feel like running, let's walk."

Before I could object, he wrapped the phone cord around my wrist and off we went.

It was almost curfew in the park, but there were still a lot of people heading for the exits and the parking lot. They created a myriad of distractions that made it hard for me to stay lined up with Leonard as we walked along the path.

Just as I was about to call a halt to this nonsense, I could hear the regular cadence of a group of runners approaching us from behind. Their footfalls pounded the path, and I could hear the length and power in their strides. These were some great runners.

Leonard said sheepishly, "Wouldn't you know it. Here comes the Tulsa Running Team."

There were a few shouted insults hurled toward Leonard and me from the lead runners. I heard, "Make way for the Midnight Runner."

And someone sneered, "This must be the blind leading the blind."

Another declared, "That blind guy sure has an old seeing eye dog."

Just when I thought the onslaught was over, I heard the last runner in the line slide to a stop and say loud enough for everyone to hear, "Hey, Ryan, I really enjoy your spot on the running team. It's nice that we have a real runner in the number eight position instead of an old has-been."

I said to Leonard under my breath, "Just keep walking and ignore them."

It was too much for Leonard to take, and his anger spilled out as he yelled, "Viktor Fulmer, you wouldn't even be on this team if your brother wasn't the captain. And in my day, not only would you have not been on the team, you couldn't even have carried the water."

Viktor Fulmer laughed derisively and shot back, "Well, this isn't your day anymore. In fact, it hasn't been your day for a long, long time. I think you're one of those has-beens who never was."

One of the other running team members called out, "Viktor, let's go. There's no use standing around here with a decrepit old man and a pathetic blind cripple. Do you know I heard Leonard screwed up, and the blind guy fell down the bank into the river?"

The whole team laughed uproariously as the insult continued. "Now they can barely walk on the path, much less run."

Inspiration can come from the most amazing places. As I absorbed the insults and contemplated the assertion I would never run again, I did the only thing a guy that has been where I have been could do. I ran.

For the first few steps, I was pulling Leonard by the phone cord before he caught up and matched my stride.

Leonard said, "I wasn't sure you were going to wait for me."

I responded loud enough for the whole running team to hear, "Well, Leonard, I knew these clowns would either get out of our way, or I would run over them, and it really didn't matter much to me which one happened."

I heard one of the team members mutter something as Leonard and I passed, but a few more strides, and we were running side by side, leaving them farther and farther behind. I knew I wasn't in shape, but I didn't want to slow our pace until we were out of sight of the running team, so I pushed it until we reached the bridge.

When I could hear the cars echoing far above us, I drew to a halt, bent over with my hands on my knees, and tried to get some air into my lungs.

When I finally caught my breath, I put my arm around Leonard and said, "Well, partner, my wind's not very good, my knees are sore, and my right ankle is protesting, but we're running again."

Leonard inquired, "Jake, what happened back there? One minute we're walking with those guys all around us, and the next minute, you're running like you were before the accident."

I thought for a minute and responded, "Leonard, I didn't care so much what they thought about me, because, frankly, I was feeling that same way about myself, but when they started saying things to you, I couldn't take it. So before I even thought about it, I was running."

Leonard laughed and elbowed me in the ribs, declaring, "So, as I understand this, when you were sitting around thinking, you couldn't do much, but when you quit thinking, you succeeded."

I returned Leonard's elbow to the ribs and said, "I'm not sure I like the way that sounds."

We both laughed, and as we walked back along the river, I realized my whole life had been a struggle between my thoughts controlling me, and me controlling my thoughts.

I wasn't 100 per cent yet, but I knew that the Midnight Runner was back.

Chapter Thirty Three

Franklin had already left for downtown Perkins to try to get a handle on Walter Grovner and why he might be pursuing Monica's grandmother's property.

I continued studying the relief map in hopes that the answer to our current quandary might magically appear. In my many years of experience in the lost and found business, I have never seen such an answer magically appear, but hope does still spring eternal.

Monica had gotten the laptop computer out of the Rolls Royce before Franklin had departed. She was in the midst of getting booted up and connected to the Internet. Being computer illiterate, I have no concept of what it means to be booting up and connecting to the Internet, but it sounds impressive, so I like to use the phrase whenever possible.

Monica set a cell phone next to me on the dining room table, and she arranged herself behind the laptop computer across the table from me. When the silence from the other end of the table reached a certain point, I knew Monica was ready, willing, and able for instructions.

I wasn't sure where to begin, so I did what I normally do which is to say the first thing that comes to mind.

"Monica, see if you can find real estate listings around your grandmother's property, and then check some online newspaper listings from six months or a year ago."

I was hoping her research would show a spike in property values around Lucinda Balfour's home.

Meanwhile, I prepared to do what I do best. As a blind person, there are a number of things I can't do at all. Driving a car and flying an airplane come to mind, although I have tried both since losing my sight. It's undoubtedly not a wise practice, and even so, I had a sighted person next to me to assist as needed.

Then there are a number of things I can do, but I have to go about them differently than sighted people. I can walk with the aid of my cane or read books if they are available in an audio format.

I have always found it interesting that when I could read books with my eyes, I never did much reading. But after losing my sight, I listen to an audio book virtually every day thanks to a high-speed tape player.

But as a blind person, there are a few things that I can do just as well—if not better—than a sighted person. Among these things would be using the telephone as a research or investigative tool.

Throughout the years, I have found that people are less threatened and therefore more willing to talk with me on the phone than they would be in person. I have found that sighted people can pick up subtle non-verbal clues when having a face-to-face conversation; however, I have found that there are similar audio clues that exist when you're utilizing the telephone.

After a few calls, I discovered that Perkins Realty was the top agency in the area. I wanted a leading agency because, generally, they will have people that specialize in specific parts of the market, and they are also usually big enough to have a receptionist answering the phone for everyone instead of having real estate agents answer the phone themselves.

I have found that secretaries and receptionists are valuable allies in doing research. They typically know everything that goes on within the entire operation and, unfortunately, they are not always treated with respect; therefore, when I call and show them respect in the midst of a polite conversation, they often can become a storehouse of information.

On the third ring, the phone was answered. "Perkins Realty. This is Shelly."

She had a distinctive accent that let me know it was likely that she had grown up in this part of Tennessee.

I began, "Shelly, how are you today?"

"Fine," she said warily as normally the only people who care about how she might be are salespeople.

I allayed her fears as I responded, "That's great. My name is Durward Stine. I'm in town for a few days representing some financial interests in New England who are seeking to acquire blocks of property in this area."

Her tone brightened significantly as she asked, "How may I help you, Mr. Stine?"

It was time to present the bait and prepare to set the hook.

I explained, "The parties I represent have significant resources, and they have become aware of the outlying area where property values are really heating up. They want to tie up a lot of acreage in that entire corridor."

After a long pause, Shelly stated, "I'm not sure what you're talking about."

I took on a conspiratorial tone and said, "Shelly, I appreciate getting to deal with a real professional like you. I understand why you would say that, but we're right on top of the situation. The people I represent don't miss anything."

Shelly seemed baffled as she said, "Mr. Stine, I really, truly don't know what you're talking about. If you could tell me what area you're interested in, I could put you through to our agent that specializes in that location."

I assumed an indignant, self-important tone and demanded, "Shelly, if you're not going to help me, let me speak with the owner."

I was on hold an interminable length of time, or it may just have seemed that way, because the Perkins Realty on-hold music is provided by a local country and western station that was doing a tribute to Slim Whitman and his yodeling tunes.

Finally, I heard a deep, authoritative voice announce, "This is Clarence Grubb. Can I help you?"

I gave him my line about representing some investors in the northeast.

He asked warily, "Mr. Stine, if you're in town representing people from the northeast, why are you calling from an Oklahoma area code?"

Caller I.D. has changed the way we have to work in the Dyer Straits Lost and Found business, but I was ready for his accusing question and responded, "Mr. Grubb, the parties that I represent have regional people across the country and around the world. When they heard about the coming boom in real estate around here, they sent me over from Tulsa."

He stated firmly, "Well, whoever your people are, they got some bad information, because any trends in real estate around here are not good ones."

I mumbled, "Thanks," and hung up.

Next, I fell back on a tried and true source for information as I called the Perkins Weekly Journal. A harried voice answered, "Journal."

I responded, "Yes, I need to talk to whoever handles your business section."

My inquiry was answered with laughter as he said, "That would be me. Whether it's business, politics, sports scores, obituaries, or news from the garden club, I'm your guy."

I explained, "I'm with the National News Wire Service, and we want to get a feel for the real estate boom you're having down there as part of a national story."

More laughter emanated from the phone receiver as he replied, "I have no idea what you're talking about, but if you're looking for a real estate boom, you'll have to go elsewhere."

I probed further. "Obviously, you are not in-the-know. Who could I talk to that would be up to speed on this?"

"Look, buddy," he replied indignantly. "If there's anybody up to speed around here, it's me, and you don't have a clue what you're talking about."

I was formulating how to present a weak apology when he hung up on me.

Monica's Internet search had confirmed my findings.

I had told Franklin and Monica that we had two threads that we could pull on to see how this mess might unravel. One of them had just broken off. I hoped Franklin would have better results than I did.

Chapter Thirty Four

Leonard Ryan and I were running almost every day. Our speed and distance were approaching the level we had achieved before the accident.

As we were running side by side on a gorgeous night, I was enjoying all of the sounds, smells, and textures of Tulsa's River Park stretching along the downtown area. It was hard to imagine that there had been a time just after the accident that I was terrified to even walk into the park and sit on the bench—in much the same way as when I was sitting on that bench, it was impossible to imagine ever running again.

As my fitness level continued to improve, I found that Leonard and I could carry on a conversation while we ran. We talked about everything and nothing in particular, and sometimes, we just ran silently—connected by Monica's pilfered telephone cord and a special bond of friendship building between us.

Without establishing a formal rule or policy, Leonard and I had begun alternating who selected the routes we would run each night. It was Leonard's night, and as we passed under the bridge, he decided to go straight. It dawned on me that we were approaching a section of trail that we hadn't been on in quite some time.

Then it hit me. We were rapidly approaching the very spot where I had stepped off the path, tumbled down the boulders, and fallen into the river. I did the only thing that came to my mind as I focused on the accident which was to stop, dead in my tracks, right there on the path. I stood as still as a statue and was terrified to even move.

Leonard seemed cruel and out of character as he declared, "Viktor

Fulmer was right about you. You never were a good runner, and you're going to be helpless from now on."

I couldn't imagine this person I considered to be my friend saying something like that. I decided to take my anger out on Leonard Ryan by running him into the ground.

I took off running at a suicidal pace and was gratified to feel the tension in the phone cord behind me. Leonard was having a hard time keeping up, but slowly the tension began to lesson as Leonard moved up beside me and matched my pace stride-for-stride.

I ran until I thought I could go no further.

I began pulling ahead of Leonard again, and just before I was ready to give up on our battle of wills, Leonard hissed, "Enough!"

We both collapsed onto the grass beside the path and panted until, eventually, my heart rate slowed and my breathing returned to something close to normal.

Leonard rolled over and stated emphatically, "Jacob Dyer, you are 100 per cent back to normal—physically and mentally—and you could compete with almost anybody."

I decided it wasn't the best time to tell Leonard that he called a halt just a few paces before I would have collapsed myself.

My anger had cooled, but the sting of his words still affected me as I said, "I didn't deserve what you said back there."

Leonard replied with a wise and measured tone, "Jacob, you're about as good a friend as I've ever had, and I want you to know you deserve everything I did and more. I would not have done what I did if I didn't care about you as much as I do."

I shot back, "Does that include insulting your friend?"

"Yes," Leonard patiently answered. "When an insult is the only thing that would take your mind off of the accident, it's what I had to do. I found out many years ago when I went from being nobody to becoming a world class runner that your mind can only focus on one thing at a time. If you think about the finish line, you can't focus on the pain. On the other hand, if you worry about the other competitors instead of running your own race, you've already lost in your mind before the competition begins."

I thought about his words and realized how much emotional energy it had taken for Leonard Ryan to do what he had done for me. I expressed the only emotion I felt.

"Thank you, Leonard."

Then I laughed uproariously, and Leonard inquired, "What is so funny?"

I got my laughter under control and replied, "Leonard, I appreciate what you did for me, and I know why you did it. I'm just hoping that someday, I can return the favor and insult you for your own good."

Every trial we face in life and every ordeal we overcome provides its own right of passage. There is a point in time when we have passed the test and dealt with the situation. Then comes the day when we know we can put it in our past. And, finally, we reach the summit and are certain we will never go back again.

I wasn't sure where the Midnight Runner or Jacob Dyer were going, but I knew it was forward and not backward.

We begin dying when we realize that our best days are behind us, then we only exist by dwelling on the past. We begin living when we know our best days are in the future, then we are ready to seize every day and every moment.

Chapter Thirty Five

Monica and I spent the remainder of the afternoon sitting on the deck enjoying the stream below and the wonderful surroundings of the Trail's End Resort. There is something about spending quiet, comfortable time with a beautiful woman that makes you feel better about yourself and the world in general.

I was partaking of a German beer I am particularly fond of along with a Dominican cigar with an exquisite flavor. Monica was enjoying her favorite food and beverage combination including chilled champagne and fresh strawberries.

She filled in more of the details about her life in Perkins, Tennessee. It has always been amazing to me that you can know a person better than you know yourself, but then you can travel to a place or learn about a time that was significant in their life, and it completes more of the picture you have of that special person.

When her monologue reached a natural ending place, I asked, "Monica, how come you've never told me about all of this before?"

She sighed, sipped her champagne, and replied, "I guess I was ashamed of who I was and where I'm from. Deep down, I really wondered if you would accept me if you knew about all of the warts and blemishes in my past."

I replied incredulously, "You've got to be kidding! Do you really imagine there's anything I could learn about you that would make any difference? I know who you are. Where you come from, and who you were, are just trivial details."

"It's hard to understand unconditional acceptance," Monica mused.

I explained, "Monica, if you can accept me with all of my obvious flaws and shortcomings, how could you even imagine I couldn't accept you?"

She said, "Jacob, I've never seen you that way. I've always thought you were simply amazing, and you made my life wonderful."

I chuckled and replied, "Well, I've never seen you at all, and I *know* you've made my life amazing and wonderful."

Both of us fell silent, and we seemed to be willing to leave all of the emotion where it was. Introspection is not like a curtain you simply open or close to reveal or hide everything. It is more like an onion that offers you layer upon layer to be peeled away one at a time, slowly revealing what is beneath.

It was becoming cool on the deck as early evening approached. We went inside and started a fire in the fireplace. We were just settling down at the table when Franklin returned.

He greeted Monica and me and sat at the table. As usual, he waited for my signal, so I said, "Well, Franklin, we struck out here. I simply can't find any evidence that the value of Mrs. Balfour's property has increased or any reason why it should be more attractive all of a sudden. I sure hope you've got something."

Franklin's sniff was not encouraging. He began. "Sir, under the guise of doing research into a distant cousin's family tree, I was able to explore quite a bit of the sordid background of Walter Grovner, Esquire."

As Monica began typing notes on the laptop computer, she asked, "So whaddaya got, Frankie?"

Monica is the only human being allowed to use that moniker, so Franklin offered a satisfied rumble and reported, "Walter Grovner had an undistinguished educational background, and his professional career has not improved the situation. He is what I believe you would call an ambulance chaser. Brief inquiries in the legal community ranged from derisive to verbiage I will not repeat in front of Miss Monica."

Monica giggled, and I stated, "I'm sure it's nothing she hasn't heard before."

Franklin continued, "There are only two recent developments of note that anyone was willing to offer. First was his sudden and unexpected appointment to the parole board. This seems to be some type of political payoff and resulted in his brother's early release from the penitentiary."

Monica slapped the table and declared, "So that's how he did it."

Franklin sniffed and said, "Yes, miss. A most unsavory business."

Monica was typing her notes into the computer, and I was tracing the relief map of the area as I considered how Walter Grovner's appointment to the parole board could possibly impact our situation. I could see no connection, so I prodded Franklin.

"You mentioned a second point."

"Yes," Franklin reported. "This is a most recent development and came to me via means I would prefer not to articulate unless completely necessary; however, it seems that another huge political payoff has resulted in Walter Grover, attorney at law, being appointed to the Tennessee Highway Commission."

Initially I was underwhelmed about Franklin's second and final point, but I listened patiently and continued tracing the contours of the relief map with my fingers as Franklin told us that Walter's appointment to the highway commission would not even be public until next month.

Sometimes in life, there are a disconnected jumble of facts and circumstances that litter the landscape. There seems to be no order or continuity to anything. This was in my mind as I traced the V of electrical tape on the map representing the two major highways and then touched the square of tape representing Monica's grandmother's acreage.

Instantly, the world came into sharp focus. I wasn't sure what we were going to do, but I finally knew why we were here and where we were going to begin.

Chapter Thirty Six

I was lounging in my leather chair with my feet up on the desk, smoking a wonderful cigar that had been handcrafted by an artist in Ecuador. The warm breeze and the sounds of the city were drifting in through my open window when Monica entered my 14th floor sanctuary and perched herself on the edge of my desk in the spot reserved for casual or personal conversations.

"Jacob," she declared, "since we have cleared two cases this week, and since we have been working way too hard, I have taken the initiative to plan an afternoon outing."

I feigned a stern protest and inquired, "What makes you think you can just plan such an outing when I'm in charge of everything around here?"

Monica laughed and replied, "You may be in charge of everything around here, but sometimes you forget that I'm in charge of *you*."

I leaned back, puffed on my cigar, and admitted, "Sometimes I forget that."

"Well, Jacob, you're lucky you've got me here to remind you I'm in charge and to plan your outings," she replied.

I inquired, "Well, are you going to tell me about this outing you have planned?"

Monica announced, "First, you and Leonard Ryan are going to go for a wonderful, invigorating late afternoon run which will conclude at a designated picnic table at the River Park where I have arranged a sunset dinner befitting this occasion."

"That all sounds great, but while you may be in charge of me, you're not in charge of Leonard Ryan, and he has a brokerage business to run that certainly involves him working this afternoon."

Monica sighed and spoke as if she were addressing a misbehaving child who didn't understand the rules.

"Jacob, Jacob, Jacob. After all of these years, do you think I would plan one of my patented afternoon outings culminating in a sunset picnic dinner extravaganza without making all of the arrangements, including contacting Leonard Ryan?"

I laughed and said, "I'm sorry I doubted you. When do the festivities commence?"

Monica stood up and spoke as she moved toward the door. "If you leave now, you can just barely make it home in time to change into your running clothes and meet Leonard at the bench."

As my cane and I made our way through the outer office to the lobby door of Dyer Straits Lost and Found, Monica left me with two parting thoughts: "Jacob, don't be late," and "Thank God for me."

As I rode down the 14 floors to the lobby of the Derrick Building in the creaky, antiquated elevator, I hoped I wouldn't be late, and I did have a moment to thank God for Monica.

As I exited the building, my friend Leroy Small shouted a question from his newsstand. "Hey, Jacob, are you only working half days now?"

"No way," I explained. "Monica planned something this afternoon without telling me beforehand."

Leroy laughed loudly and called toward my retreating back as I rapidly walked away, "Jacob, you can thank God Almighty that you've got her."

I traversed the eight blocks from my office to my Plaza Tower apartment building and was just exiting the elevator on the 22nd floor, when I had one of my frequent encounters in the hallway with my next door neighbor, Linda Taylor.

Ms. Linda Taylor is a mysterious fixture in the Plaza Tower apartment building. Physical descriptions of her range from "drop dead gorgeous" to "out of this world." While I cannot testify in detail to that personally,

I do know that gentlemen in my building tend to develop breathing problems when she's present, and the population around the swimming pool seems to quadruple when she makes an appearance in her barely discernable swimsuit.

I remember a time when Franklin had come to pick me up when I was out at the pool during one of Linda's appearances. I asked Franklin to give me his personal opinion on her swimsuit.

He assured me, "Sir, it is quite memorable, and I feel certain there is no wasted fabric."

As I made my way hurriedly down the hall to my apartment, still hoping to be on time for my run with Leonard, Linda purred, "Hey, Jake, you got time for a drink?"

"No," I explained. "I've got to meet a friend in the park for a six mile run."

Linda giggled and declared, "I've always heard the key to exercise is to get your heart rate in the target zone. What do you think, Jake?"

As I fumbled for my keys, I said, "I don't know."

She responded, "Well, maybe we can explore that sometime."

Linda Taylor never seems to do any work or pursue any profession, but she's always expensively dressed and jewelry-laden and drives a high-priced sports car. Her means of financial support have long been a source of conjecture and innuendo in the apartment building.

Her ongoing interest in me has always made me a bit uncomfortable, because I've never been quite certain whether her intentions are personal or professional.

I made it to our designated park bench and folded up my cane just as Leonard Ryan arrived. We each attached the well-worn telephone cord to our wrist and started running at a slow, comfortable pace.

I began, "It's good to see you Leonard. When did Monica get in touch with you about this little outing?"

"She called me yesterday," he responded.

I said, "I hope she didn't twist your arm. Monica is kind of hard to say no to."

Leonard laughed and said, "She didn't twist my arm, and it never occurred to me to say no to Monica. In fact, if she ever gets tired of you, I would hire her to be a financial broker for me in a heartbeat."

Leonard and I ran comfortably and picked up the pace to a very respectable six minutes per mile.

As we turned to cross the bridge, Leonard announced, "Just three more miles until we meet Monica with the refreshments."

I assured Leonard, "The word *refreshments* doesn't even begin to cover what's in store for you."

Chapter Thirty Seven

I pounded the table and shouted, "I've got it!"
The room fell silent as I realized I had caught both Monica and Franklin off guard with my unexpected shouting and pounding.

Finally, Monica broke the silence. "Jake, I'm glad you've got it. Maybe you'd like to tell Franklin and me what you've got and why you're so happy about it."

I replied, "Instead of explaining it to you, I'll ask Franklin to get one more piece of electrical tape and put it on the area map at the opening of the sideways V connecting the two highways at the closest exits to Perkins."

I heard Franklin tear off a section of electrical tape, and as he arranged it on the map as I described, I heard a profound and victorious rumble emanate from Franklin.

Monica looked over my shoulder and declared, "Jacob, it goes right through the edge of Gram's property. If that were a highway, they would have to pay Gram for some of her property, and the rest of the lower 40 acres would be right on the highway."

I announced, "Now that we know why they want the property, we need to figure out what we're going to do about it."

The seed of a plan was beginning to germinate in my mind, and I knew from past experience that I shouldn't force it but, instead, just let it grow on its own.

We had determined that it would be best for Monica and her grandmother to move into the cabin while Franklin and I took up residence in Lucinda Balfour's home without Cleve Grovner knowing about the switch.

As evening was approaching and it would soon be fully dark so that we could make the housing switch, unnoticed, I declared, "Gang, we are going to bait a trap designed to get Monica and her grandmother out of this predicament and get the bad guys what they deserve. Since it's no longer important that we hide the connection between us, I suggest we have dinner at The Coffee Cup Café before we head out to meet Monica's grandmother."

Franklin signified his agreement with a rumble as he headed out to get the car started. Monica took my arm, and we settled into the Rolls Royce.

We must have made quite an impression as we got out of the car and entered The Coffee Cup Café, because the dinner patrons fell silent as we settled into our booth.

Stella, our waitress from our previous visit to the café, approached the table and spoke, "It's good to see you, Mona, and I'm glad you boys are back. What can I get for ya?

We ordered dinner, and Monica excused herself to visit the ladies room and pick up a newspaper. She was stifling laughter as she returned to our booth.

I inquired, "So, what's so funny, Monica?"

She explained, "Well, Stella—who I've known since grade school—came into the lady's room to warn me about you guys. It seems you two were in here just recently, but you were looking for another girl named Monica. She said you were throwing around a lot of money, and everybody thinks you may be involved in organized crime."

I joined in with Monica's laughter, but Franklin only offered a brief sniff as his response.

The dinner exceeded my expectations—partially due to a decent short-order cook and partially due to low expectations.

I settled the bill and gave Stella a tip sufficient to keep the organized crime rumors going.

We left The Coffee Cup Café in full darkness and headed for Lucinda Balfour's property. As Franklin piloted the Rolls Royce to follow Monica's directions, she gave us a running travelogue description of the area.

When we were within a quarter mile of the driveway, Franklin turned off the headlights so we could not be spotted from the ridge. The running lights were sufficient for Franklin to maneuver the Rolls down the driveway and drift to a stop next to Monica's sports car. Franklin opened the back door, and Monica and I stepped out. It was strange to visit this place for the first time that had meant so much to Monica throughout her life.

People who live in the city or even the suburbs can forget how quiet it is in the country. The silence almost has a sound of its own. The lack of noise is somehow audible, and it causes one to strain to pick up sounds at the distant edge of what can be heard.

The front door creaked open, and a pleasant voice called from the porch.

"Come on in, child, and introduce me to your friends."

Monica took my arm, and we walked up the three steps onto the porch.

Monica made the introductions. "Gram, this is Franklin, and this is Jacob."

Franklin intoned, "Madam, it is, indeed, both a pleasure and an honor to make your acquaintance."

I added, "Mrs. Balfour, it is great to meet you."

She hugged Franklin and me as if we were her grandchildren, and she welcomed us into her home and served tea and cookies at the kitchen table.

Monica described, "The original part of this log home was built almost 200 years ago. It's been added onto several times throughout the last few generations of my family. Gram keeps it and the property spotless."

After we finished our tea and cookies, Monica and her grandmother showed Franklin and me all around the house that would be our home for the duration of this matter.

Franklin took Monica's and her grandmother's packed bags out to the car, and we all followed him outside. Mrs. Balfour gave us a brief tour and description of the property surrounding her house. As we walked, she apologized that it was so dark. Franklin told her that it was fine, and I assured her it made no difference to me.

Mrs. Balfour sounded embarrassed as she said, "Mr. Dyer, I'm sorry. I didn't mean..."

Monica interjected, "Gram, don't worry. He always says things like that. If you don't pay any attention to him, he'll eventually shut up."

Mrs. Balfour had a sizeable garden next to the house with a lone scarecrow keeping vigil on the area. Her voice quivered as she showed us the spot where she had buried her dog, Duke, that had been shot. She explained the cattle that had been killed had been buried on the back of the property.

As we walked toward the driveway, she pointed out the light on top of the ridge where Cleve Grovner's trailer was situated.

Franklin opened the driver's door of the Rolls Royce for Monica to slide in. Then he opened the passenger door for Mrs. Balfour. This was a rare occurrence as no one drives the Rolls Royce other than Franklin.

As Monica's grandmother settled into the passenger's seat, she declared, "This is quite a rig."

The fact that Franklin rumbled in response to her questionable description of the Rolls was a sign of the respect he had for Monica's grandmother.

Monica announced, "Don't worry, Frankie. I'll take good care of your baby and look forward to when you're back here driving, and I'm in my normal spot."

Monica drove away, only using the running lights until she was well out of sight of the trailer on the ridge.

Franklin and I stood in the driveway and felt the silence close in around us.

Franklin proclaimed, "Sir, anyone that's less than civil to that precious lady has simply got to be dealt with."

I agreed.

Chapter Thirty Eight

As Leonard and I rapidly approached the designated time and place of Monica's picnic extravaganza, we were running comfortably when Leonard suddenly gasped and said, "Oh my!"

I immediately slowed, concerned that he had twisted an ankle or otherwise injured himself when he said, "I've never seen anything like it. I had no idea."

As we jogged and then walked the remaining distance to the picnic site, we cooled down and Leonard explained, "There's a linen tablecloth with real china, silverware, and long-stemmed glasses. Ornate candles have already been lit, and there's a bottle of champagne in a silver ice bucket.

"A waiter with a tuxedo is standing by the table, and Monica is wearing a strapless black evening dress. Your Rolls Royce limo is parked near the table. The music you hear is coming from the open car windows."

I tried to sound calm as if this sort of thing was rather mundane as I replied, "Yeah, that sounds about normal."

As Leonard and I arrived at the table, my old friend—and still the world's greatest waiter—Hamid handed us each a cold glass of champagne.

I said, "Good evening, Hamid. I thought you'd be working at the Duck Club tonight."

Hamid laughed and replied, "Well, sir, I guess it would be safe to say Miss Monica made me a better offer."

Franklin rumbled a greeting and said, "Good evening, sir, and greetings to you, Mr. Ryan. I assumed that a pastoral selection from Aaron Copland might be appropriate as we are dining alfresco."

"Thank you, Franklin. It sounds perfect," I responded.

Monica directed everyone to their assigned seats and proposed a toast.

"Here's to the Midnight Runner and his faithful companion."

We clinked glasses and drank.

As Hamid served Caesar salads followed by Cornish hen and roasted vegetables, Monica asked Leonard, "So, Leonard, how's the boss doing as a runner?"

Leonard thought for a moment and said, "Actually, he's doing incredibly well. His stamina is improving every day, and if I had his kick over the last quarter mile, I'd still be competitive."

Monica seemed confused and asked, "What does that mean?"

Leonard explained, "Distance running is really like two races. There's the long haul over a great distance where the only thing that really matters is the ability to keep up a fast time mile after mile. Then there's the kick or sprint at the end of the race which can make all the difference. Jake has the ability to put on a burst of speed over the last quarter mile that is really remarkable."

Monica conjectured, "So, between the two of you, you make one champion runner."

We all laughed but, as usual, Monica was very perceptive. She has the ability to attack subjects she knows virtually nothing about and, by asking a few simple questions, she can get to the heart of the matter.

As we all finished our main course, Hamid approached Monica and inquired, "Miss, if everyone's ready, I'll prepare the grand finale."

Monica affirmed brightly, "Yes, indeed. Now would be perfect."

I heard the whoosh of flaming dessert, and as Hamid placed the dish before me, he intoned, "And may I present Bananas Foster as ordered by the lady."

The champagne, dinner, dessert, and conversation were everything they should be. As Hamid was offering brandy and cigars, I heard Leonard exclaim, "Not now."

I could hear the distress in his voice, and I asked, "What is it?"

His simple explanation said it all.

"The Tulsa Running Team."

It took a few seconds before I could hear the steady cadence of the footfalls approaching us. Then they slowed and came to a stop around our table.

The captain, Dietrich Fulmer, sneered, "What's going on here? I can't imagine what you guys have to celebrate."

Dietrich's younger brother, Viktor, who had taken Leonard's eighth position on the team, shouted, "I think they're celebrating the fact that the old goat and the blind cripple are finally giving it up."

The team laughed uproariously, and one of them knocked over the champagne bucket as he grabbed the bottle and passed it around among the team. They began picking up food and closing in on us in a threatening manner.

Finally, I heard Franklin say, in a tone that stopped everyone in their tracks, "Sir, if you lay one hand on that automobile, I will be forced to thrash you mercilessly."

As the intruders were trying to decide how seriously to take Franklin's threat, I heard a brief burst of a police siren as a car pulled up beside the limo. A door opened and then slammed, and I heard the unmistakable voice of Officer Armstrong say, "What's going on here?"

Dietrich Fulmer spoke for the running team, replying, "Officer, we were just celebrating with our friends here before those of us who are still competitive runners finish our workout."

Officer Armstrong approached, stating unequivocally, "Well, then, I suggest you start running, because it looks like the celebration's over."

As the running team members moved back toward the path to resume their run, Viktor Fulmer declared loudly enough for everyone to hear, "I can't think of anything worse than a has-been tied to a never-was by a phone cord."

Officer Armstrong stayed in place until the runners were far down the path. Then he said uncomfortably, "Well, folks, I guess it's all over."

Monica stated, "They're gone, but if I know Jacob Dyer, it's far from over."

Chapter Thirty Nine

I have always been an early riser. It comes naturally to me. When people learn I'm often up at 4:00 a.m., they gasp in shock and horror, but they don't understand it feels right to me and has allowed me to enjoy what I know as the best time of the day.

Either Franklin is an early riser as well, or he matches his internal clock to mine when it is necessary; therefore, we found ourselves seated at Mrs. Balfour's kitchen table drinking coffee at 4:30 the next morning.

Monica had sent me an email that I listened to as a digital audio message on my cell phone. She wanted to let me know that she and her grandmother were safely settled in the cabin at the Trail's End Resort. I couldn't help but take note of the fact that Monica had sent the email only three hours earlier, at 1:30 a.m.

Monica is, most assuredly, not an early riser.

Franklin was quiet, knowing that I was trying to formulate a plan of action. We sipped coffee and ate some bagels that Franklin had toasted for us.

Finally, I suggested, "Franklin, let's go outside and wander around a bit and see what comes to mind."

As we stepped onto the porch, the depth of the silence struck me again. I found it easier than normal to follow Franklin as we explored the property.

Monica's sports car was parked in the driveway, and Franklin reported that the light on the trailer atop the ridge was still burning brightly. As it was still fully dark at this hour, I knew we couldn't be observed by Cleve Grovner and, in any event, I assumed he was probably passed out from a late night of drinking as Monica had described.

We walked through Mrs. Balfour's orderly and well-tended garden. Franklin described the peaceful and tranquil setting, giving me a feel for our surroundings and filling in the picture in my mind.

Franklin sniffed several times, so I inquired, "Something wrong?"

"Well, sir," he responded. "I am far from an expert on scarecrows, but in the midst of such an impressive garden, this character seems out of place, disheveled, and a bit disreputable."

Franklin described the hunched-over figure of a scarecrow looking rather forlorn, clad in a tattered and moth-eaten topcoat.

I explained, "Franklin, the purpose of a scarecrow is to scare away the crows, not to make a fashion statement."

Franklin sniffed and said, "Well, sir, this fellow seems capable of scaring away either man or beast."

As we moved back around to the front of the house, I announced, "Franklin, I don't have any really great ideas, so I guess we ought to just take the bull by the horns. Why don't you get Monica's car keys?"

Franklin rumbled and replied, "Very well, sir. I think it's about time this bull was firmly grasped by his horns."

Franklin expertly fired up Monica's sports car, and we backed out of the driveway and made our way up the rutted country road toward the trailer on the ridge.

Franklin sniffed decisively as he pulled off the road and onto a rough gravel driveway. He killed the engine and described the setting.

"Sir, we have a ramshackle trailer displaying ample rust, fronted by a rickety set of stairs. The front yard has an odd collection of rubbish and castaway items which includes an old washing machine, assorted tires, an automobile transmission, and a horrific velour sofa with a sunflower pattern that is sitting at the far edge of the yard. Broken trash bags are strewn about, and all considered, it is most revolting."

I felt I had a pretty good picture of the area in my mind, so I said,

"Well, Franklin, there's no time like the present. Let's see if anybody's home."

As I opened my door to get out, I chuckled and said, "Franklin, hit the horn a couple of times. Cleve Grovner may not normally be up and about at 6:00 a.m."

The horn sounded, and we stood in complete silence for several minutes until the front door of the trailer banged open, and a gruff voice said, "Who are you, and what do you want?"

I responded cheerily, "Just the type of questions that go directly to the crux of the matter."

I heard him shuffle on the porch and walk down the two steps to the yard.

He said, "I'm Cleve Grovner, and you're on my property."

I replied, "You may be Cleve Grovner, but the ownership of this property is a matter of debate."

He shot back accusingly, "Why are you driving my wife's car?"

"I believe that would be your ex-wife," I corrected him.

He roared, "I'm going to ask you one last time who you are and what you want."

Franklin spoke for all to hear. "Sir, excuse me for interrupting, but if this rather unkempt gentleman should raise the barrel of that rifle even a fraction of an inch, I am curious as to whether you would prefer I put a 9mm round in his left eye, his right eye, or simply between his eyes."

I regulated my breathing and tried to respond as if I had this type of conversation every day and droned, "Franklin, it's early in the morning, and there's no need to get fancy about it. If he twitches, just put a round right between his eyes. We blind guys are just a little sensitive about damaging even a lowlife's eyes."

"Very well, sir," Franklin intoned.

Cleve Grovner laughed and spat, "That's pretty big talk, but I don't see any guns anywhere."

I heard a slight shift and brief rustle of Franklin's jacket to my left. I knew from past experience that in the blink of an eye, Cleve Grovner found himself looking straight down the barrel of a very steady 9mm automatic handgun.

Grovner cleared his throat nervously but recovered somewhat, saying, "That's a fancy draw, but it doesn't mean you can shoot that thing. I'm over a hundred feet away, uphill. That's a pretty tall order for a handgun."

I tried to sound bored and annoyed as I said, "Franklin, put a round in the middle of one of those sunflowers on the ugly sofa."

Before the last word was fully out of my mouth, I heard the crack of Franklin's 9mm pistol.

Franklin calmly reported, "Just as you would expect, sir."

I observed, "Well, now we all know my colleague can shoot. How are you with that rifle?"

I heard the rifle bark, and Franklin sniffed derisively and stated, "Well, sir, he did at least hit the sofa."

I announced, "Round one goes to the dapper British gentleman with the quick and highly accurate handgun over the degenerate hillbilly with the errant rifle."

Cleve Grovner roared, "You jerks get off of my property and out of the county, or my brother and I will..."

"Your brother and you will do what?" I asked.

Grovner sputtered unintelligibly so I interrupted and explained, "This property and the property below all belong to Mrs. Lucinda Balfour as it has been in her family for many generations. It was deeded to you for the express purpose of insuring that her granddaughter would have it; therefore, I suggest you clear out and find somewhere else to go and someone else to bother."

Grovner threatened, "We'll take care of you both, along with the old lady and my pathetic wife."

I let my anger boil to the surface and stated for the record, "Cleve Grovner, you're not able to take care of yourself, much less both of us, and if anything happens to your ex-wife or her grandmother, you will get blamed for everything.

"You've already killed several of her cattle along with her dog, and you've publicly threatened an old lady whose family has been a part of this community for two centuries. How long do you think it will be before they point the finger at an ex-con who's out on a questionable parole?"

Grovner laughed vindictively and spat, "My brother will take care of you guys."

I moved toward the car, and Franklin followed suit. I delivered my parting shot. "Your brother's a lightweight idiot that won't bear up to the most basic scrutiny. He will leave you holding the bag, and don't forget, if anything happens to anybody, they'll come for you, and Tennessee still has the death penalty. By the way, we already know all about the highway."

I slammed my car door and signaled for Franklin to get us out of there.

As he drove, he rumbled and declared, "Sir, I believe we have most decisively thrown the gauntlet down. Mr. Grovner is standing there dumbstruck and defeated with his mouth hanging open."

Sometimes, the best way to handle someone pushing you is to push them back hard. And then there are other times when you simply step back and let them fall from the weight of their own momentum and bluster.

Chapter Forty

I slept fitfully that night as I couldn't get the image of the Tulsa Running Team ruining Monica's special dinner out of my mind. I woke even earlier than usual, feeling frustrated and out of sorts. I decided to make my way to the office and deal with it there.

As I got off the elevator and made my way down the hall toward the door of the Dyer Straits Lost and Found agency, I heard someone moving around inside my office. I was prepared to confront an intruder at this pre-dawn hour when I heard Monica call out, "It's just me, Jake."

I swung the door open and entered as Monica explained, "I had some research to do, so I got here a little early."

I laughed and responded, "Monica, this is more than a little early. In fact, when you called out to me, my first thought was you were having a late night, not an early morning."

Monica dismissed me and spoke. "Jacob, are you going to stand around and quibble about the time of day or sit down at your desk and listen to what I have discovered?"

When you don't have a choice, it's not too hard to make a decision, so I flipped the switch on the coffee maker and eased into my chair behind my desk.

Monica paced back and forth, referring to several papers she was shuffling in her hands.

"Jake, it's only 92 days until the Tulsa Metro Run. It is a 15K, officially sanctioned race, which—according to the Tulsa Running Team's website—allows a competitor to challenge for one of the eight places on the team."

She shuffled several more pages and continued. "Now, I have checked all of the stipulations with regard to entering the Tulsa Metro Run, and it clearly states that any runner with a disability can be assisted by another runner. Furthermore, if the assistance rendered would not improve the time that otherwise could be achieved by that runner, he or she is able to compete in the race."

The coffee maker had completed doing its job, so I poured my first cup of the day into my Donald Duck mug and asked, "Do you want to tell me what you're talking about?"

"Jacob Dyer," she spoke measuredly, "you obviously haven't been listening to me. Drink your coffee and try to focus. What I'm saying is that you can challenge Viktor Fulmer for his eighth spot on the Tulsa Running Team that he took away from Leonard.

"You can run in the race as a qualified participant with Leonard assisting you, because there's no way anyone could claim that that phone cord could increase your speed or improve your time."

I leaned back in my chair, completely dumbstruck by the mere thought of running along with thousands of other people in the Tulsa Metro Run while challenging a competitive runner for his place on the Tulsa Running Team.

I was just formulating the words that would help Monica understand the absurdity of what she was proposing when the outer door to the office burst open, and I heard Leonard Ryan rush in, shouting, "I thought that had to be your light I saw from the street."

Leonard slipped into one of my client chairs just as if he had been expected at this ridiculous hour and was arriving for an appointment.

I observed, "This is turning into a regular sunrise prayer meeting. Good morning, Leonard."

Leonard spoke as if he hadn't heard me. "Jacob, after that deal yesterday, I couldn't stand it, so I made some calls last night and got a few people out of bed. I may not be the runner I used to be, but I'm still a big deal in the competitive running world."

Monica slid into the other client chair silently as if she anticipated something of great interest.

Leonard continued. "I've got it all worked out. It's 12 weeks or so until the Tulsa Metro Run. You and I can compete by running in tandem just as we normally do, and you can challenge Viktor Fulmer for the place he took from me on the Tulsa Running Team."

I protested, "You can't honestly believe that's possible."

Leonard sounded hurt and forlorn as he pleaded, "Jake, I know I'm not near what I used to be, but I will promise you—with everything I have inside of me—if you will trust me and do this, I will put you right on Viktor Fulmer's tail with a quarter of a mile to go or I will die trying. So help me God."

He slammed his open palm on my desk.

I shot back defensively, "Leonard, I love you and everything you've done for me. I'm not questioning *your* ability. I'm doubting my own."

Monica spoke for me. "Leonard, you arrange all the paperwork and get the ball rolling. I know you can get Jacob even with Viktor Fulmer, and I would bet everything—in an even race over the last quarter mile— Jake will run him down."

It seemed impossible, but I knew it couldn't be any other way.

Chapter Forty One

Franklin pulled Monica's sports car back into Mrs. Balfour's driveway after our little early morning visit to Cleve Grovner.

I exclaimed, "Franklin, if you poke a stick into a hornet's nest, something is bound to come out."

A brief rumble signaled his agreement, and I continued. "It's a good way to get all the hornets moving, but you've got to be sure you don't get stung in the process."

Franklin inquired, "With that in mind, how should we proceed, sir?"

As we walked into the house, I said, "Franklin, I believe we're going to have a visitor this morning. I suggest we enjoy a second cup of coffee on the front porch, and you may want to be cleaning your pistol when our guest arrives."

Franklin actually chuckled and replied, "Yes, sir. And since it is expeditious that I be cleaning my weapon in front of our guest, may I suggest I also take the opportunity to clean Mrs. Balfour's shot gun she has in the gun rack next to the door."

I responded, "Franklin, a good houseguest and a responsible gun owner could do no less."

Franklin and I were, indeed, enjoying the morning sipping our coffee sitting on the front porch when I heard a vehicle approach on the road.

Franklin described, "Sir, a late model four-door sedan is turning into the driveway. There seems to be only one occupant of the vehicle."

The car pulled to a stop, and the engine was turned off. There was an uncomfortable few moments of silence before I heard a car door open and then slam shut.

Franklin spoke loud enough for only me to hear. "Sir, a rather short, rumpled man is approaching slowly. He is wearing a ghastly polyester brown suit and sporting an improbable toupee."

"I'll bet you another cup of coffee we're about to meet Walter Grovner," I declared.

Franklin merely sniffed, and the figure walking up the driveway called, "Good morning, gentlemen. I am Walter Grovner."

Franklin and I just sat and sipped our coffee, which created an uncomfortable silence.

Finally, Walter Grovner spoke again. "I was hoping to have a conversation with you gentlemen regarding a matter of mutual interest."

We maintained our silence, and Walter inquired, "Might I know who I am addressing?"

I responded, "I would think if you want to talk with us about a matter of mutual interest, you would know who we are."

He laughed uncomfortably and continued, "Well, then, I will assume that you are Mr. Jacob Dyer, and your colleague would be the gentleman known as Franklin. The two of you are creating quite a stir around here."

I said, "I'm glad to know we've been noticed."

I heard Franklin break open the shotgun. Walter Grovner took a quick step to the side and shouted, "I'm not armed!"

Franklin merely sniffed, and I said, "I'm not either, and Franklin is a stickler for gun maintenance. He had occasion to fire his weapon earlier today to discourage a rodent. And that's all it takes for him to want to clean his gun."

Franklin chimed in, "Sir, I've always felt that one's weapon should be ready to fire at any moment one might require it."

I smiled broadly and responded, "Yes, Franklin, that's a good thing to keep in mind."

Walter Grovner stated, "Gentlemen, this is not necessary. We are all men of the world. I believe if we can simply have a meeting of the minds among us, we will find our association to be profitable for all concerned."

I addressed Franklin. "I've always found it fascinating that people spend a lot of time and money to go to law school for the purpose of clarifying and simplifying things, but when they get out, they're harder to understand than they were before."

Franklin rumbled, and I let the silence lay between us.

Finally, Walter continued. "Look, Dyer, let's drop all of the fun and games here and get down to business. Nothing in the divorce decree changes anything. My brother, Cleve, is the rightful owner of the property on the ridge and this property here as soon as the old lady dies or moves. And she hasn't been seen around here recently."

I responded, "Maybe she hasn't been seen around here because your brother has gotten in the habit of shooting his rifle down here."

He blurted out, "You can't prove that."

I laughed and said, "I probably could prove it, but I don't have to right now."

Walter Grovner moved forward and put one foot on the first porch step. Franklin snapped the shotgun closed. Grovner froze in his tracks.

His voice cracked as he asked, "Is the old lady here? Can I speak with her?"

I responded, "Where she is is none of your business, and she doesn't want to speak to you. This is still her rightful property."

Walter said, "I beg to differ. If she is not alive and well and living here, this property falls to my brother."

He moved up one step and took on a conspiratorial tone as he continued. "Gentlemen, if we simply can get together on this thing, we can all become quite wealthy. My brother and I are not greedy men, and we would be willing to share any potential profit with you. I don't really care what has happened to the old lady."

I stood, and Franklin took that moment as an opportunity to stand next to me on the porch and fire both barrels of the shotgun over Walter Grovner's head. The sound was thunderous and echoed throughout the valley.

Walter Grovner had moved several paces back down the driveway and spoke in a high-pitched wheeze.

"You can't scare me."

I laughed with all the venom I felt and said, "I think we just did scare you."

Franklin sniffed and reported, "The weapon fires perfectly, sir. It is serviceable and ready for action should we encounter any other undesirable members of the rodent family."

Walter Grovner rushed back to his car and shouted toward the porch. "You had your chance. We can deal with you and the old lady."

I yelled back, "You can't begin to deal with us, and if anything happens to Mrs. Balfour, you and your brother will go all the way down."

Walter Grovner slammed his car door, started his engine, and squealed his tires as he backed out of the driveway and rocketed down the country road.

When the silence returned to the porch, Franklin stated, "Sir, may I say, that all went quite well."

I agreed.

Chapter Forty Two

Before I knew it, I was an officially-registered competitor in the Tulsa Metro Run. The Tulsa Metro Run is a 15K race which means 9.6 miles to those of us who have not yet fully embraced or even considered the metric system.

I had never run 9.6 miles all at once, but Leonard assured me, "It won't be a problem." Those famous words have come back to haunt me several times in my life, and I was hoping this wasn't going to be another one of those occasions.

The race route would be mostly along the north and south segments of the River Park with which I was very familiar, but then the final segment of the race would move along city streets and end in the center of downtown Tulsa. This meant I would be running on streets with which I was totally unfamiliar.

Once again, Leonard assured me, "It won't be a problem."

Our training runs took on a new urgency as we had a goal in mind with a specific date attached to it. We continued running in the park after midnight, and then, at the end of each of our workouts, we carefully walked, then ran, over every inch of the route along the city streets.

Leonard had competed in the Tulsa Metro Run many times, so as the race day approached, he and I both knew the route like the proverbial backs of our hands.

I actually found myself sitting at my desk or lounging at home replaying the race route in my mind over and over. I paid particular attention to the last quarter mile of the race, because our strategy called for Leonard and me to run in tandem—attached by the phone cord—for approximately

9.3 miles and then we would disconnect the phone cord, and I would be on my own to sprint the last quarter mile or so—hopefully faster than Viktor Fulmer could.

Over the years of learning to live as a blind person, I had become comfortable without the aid of my cane or anyone's assistance navigating my office as well as my apartment. Over the weeks and months before I was to compete in the Tulsa Metro Run, I became just as familiar with the last quarter mile of the race route.

Three weeks before race day, Leonard declared, "It's time for a trial run."

I inquired, "Exactly what do you have in mind when you say *trial run?*"

Leonard explained, "Tomorrow night, you and I are going to run the entire Tulsa Metro Run at midnight. We will begin at the start line and run as if it were race day until you cross the finish line. We will time this on my stopwatch and compare our practice run to the best time Viktor Fulmer has ever posted in the Tulsa Metro Run."

This sounded good to me as I was anxious to find out how we might do against Viktor Fulmer.

I was more nervous than I thought I would be when I met Leonard at our regular park bench just before midnight. We stretched and jogged a little to get warmed up and ready for our trial race. Precisely at midnight, we shook hands.

Leonard said, "Go," and he clicked the stopwatch.

Although Leonard and I had probably run hundreds of miles along this same River Park path, it seemed different this time—simply because I knew there was a stopwatch ticking away which represented the phantom figure of my competition, Viktor Fulmer.

We completed the River Park portion of our trial run and moved onto the city streets toward downtown where the finish line would be located.

After midnight, the city streets were almost void of traffic, so we pounded along the pavement through the concrete canyons of the city.

I felt the tension growing in my heart and mind as we ran toward the exact spot when I would release the phone cord and run the last quarter mile alone. I could feel Leonard's stride becoming more labored as he struggled to keep the pace all the way to the release point.

Then it was time. Leonard veered off to the side as I released the phone cord and ran as if my life were at stake. And maybe it was.

I felt strong, and I held to a full sprint until I crossed the point where the finish line would be on race day. I walked in circles to cool down and heard Leonard clapping as he approached.

He called, "Great run, Jake. We're only 30 seconds behind Viktor Fulmer's best time."

My heart sank. I couldn't believe that we would ever be able to get a better time than we had just run.

Leonard sensed my mood and said, "It won't be a problem."

I said, "You keep saying that, but it really feels like a problem."

Leonard explained, "Jake, everybody gets an adrenalin boost on race day. There will be thousands of people running all around you, and thousands more lining the race route. It will be different because you will know it's for real. All of that together should be worth at least 30 seconds."

It didn't really make sense to me, but I had trusted Leonard Ryan over many months and many miles, so I wasn't about to start doubting him now.

Chapter Forty Three

I was having one of those fleeting thoughts in the back of my mind that told me something wasn't completely right. If you miss something when you're typing a letter, you just delete or change the part that wasn't right. If you miss something when you're dealing with people like Cleve and Walter Grovner, it can be a lot worse.

I reviewed in my mind the early morning confrontation with Cleve Grovner and the conversation and argument with his brother Walter that had taken place a few hours later. There was a fleeting wisp of a thought playing in the shadows of my mind, but I couldn't capture it and pull it into the light of day.

Sometimes when you're trying to remember something or master a mental task, you reach a point where more focus and deeper concentration won't get you anywhere. The only thing you can do is quit beating your head against the wall, and focus on something else for a while. Quite often, that which you have been seeking will pop into your consciousness while you're busy dealing with something else.

This was my hope as I called Monica at the Trail's End Resort to make sure she and her grandmother were all right and to update her on the encounters with the two Grovner brothers.

"Good morning, Jake," she answered the phone pleasantly.

I consulted my Braille watch before I answered and, as it was, indeed, a few minutes before noon, I responded, "Good morning to you, too."

She confirmed that all was well with her and her grandmother in the cabin at the resort.

I cautioned her to take extra care as the proverbial pot was heating up, and the stew would be boiling very soon.

I reconstructed the content and substance of both conversations with the Grovners to the best of my ability and recollection.

Monica sounded perplexed as she asked, "I wonder why Cleve keeps calling me his wife instead of his ex-wife? He really hates me and hasn't wanted anything to do with me since shortly after we were married."

Her question was tumbling through my mind as I remembered Walter Grovner saying: *Nothing in the divorce decree changes anything.*

Mr. Shakespeare wrote that immortal line: *Methinks thou dost protest too much.*

That fleeting wisp of a thought I had been struggling to grasp stepped out of the shadow just long enough for me to grab it.

I excitedly interrupted whatever Monica was saying to ask, "Monica, where are your divorce papers?"

After a long pause, she questioned, "My divorce papers? What in the world would you ask about that for?"

I responded, "I don't know why I'm asking, but I have a feeling that once I review them, I will have the answer to the question we should be dealing with right now."

The line was silent for several moments, then Monica spoke. "I can't say for sure, Jake, but my best guess would be they're tucked away in the file drawer next to Gram's desk there in the house."

I ended our conversation with, "Let me get back to you."

Franklin sniffed a protest when I explained he was going to have to paw through Mrs. Balfour's files to find Monica's divorce papers and then read them to me. But when I explained it was necessary to keep Monica and her grandmother safe and vanquish the bad guys, he reluctantly rumbled his approval.

After 20 minutes or so, Franklin announced, "Sir, this looks promising. There are several papers stapled together in a file marked *Divorce*. An official-looking document with the seal of the State of Tennessee has a heading that reads *Divorce Decree*."

I had Franklin wade through the entire document, word-for-word. It was literally filled with legalese, but somewhere among all of the heretofores, whereases, and to-wits, he read a beautiful phrase that clearly stated for anyone who bothered to read it: *The marital home and all contents therein, other than the personal effects of Cleve Grovner, will become the sole property of Mona Grovner. This will include the option on a 40-acre parcel of land titled to Mrs. Lucinda Balfour.*

An immense rumble of satisfaction emanated from Franklin.

I announced, "Franklin, I believe we both just earned a cold beer."

"Very good, sir," Franklin replied. "With your permission, I shall prepare us a spot of lunch to be served with the aforementioned cold beverages."

While Franklin was busy in the kitchen, I called Monica and let her know that the good guys were going to win this one. We just had to make sure that the bad guys didn't do any serious damage between now and then.

Monica was elated about the breakthrough revealed in her divorce papers. As she hung up to go tell her grandmother the good news, I sipped my cold beer and put the final touches on the plan I was formulating that would insure Cleve and Walter Grovner got everything they deserved.

Chapter Forty Four

Race day was upon us. The last several months of training had flown by. I was pleased that the fact that a blind guy would be competing in the race—tied by a phone cord to a former Olympic runner—had gone unnoticed by the media and running community.

Leonard had pulled some strings with race officials so that we wouldn't have to deal with the added pressure of reporters, photos, and interviews.

I was overwhelmed as we stood in front of the review stand erected near the start line. Leonard and I were literally swallowed in the midst of a sea of thousands of competitors. I knew there would be a lot of runners, but I had no idea it would be like this. The butterflies in my stomach were flying in formation and doing loops at the same time.

I put my hand on Leonard's elbow as my only point of reference in the noisy, shifting melee of humanity.

The mayor gave a brief welcome to everyone who would be participating in the race as well as the spectators and the many sponsors who had made the event possible. I was amazed to hear that competitors from 17 states and four foreign countries would be competing today in the Tulsa Metro Run.

Then the mayor introduced the head race official who described the myriad of rules and regulations surrounding the competition. I let most of it flow in one ear and out the other as I simply fought to remain calm in the midst of the uncomfortable environment as I anticipated the pre-race anxiety.

Finally, the official gave his last instruction, outlining how competitors would be starting in order of the race number they had been assigned, which corresponded to their best times as a runner.

He explained, "Your official time will not begin until you cross the start line which will be registered by a scanner. Then your final time will be recorded by the computer when you're scanned crossing the finish line."

I was trying to make sense of all of this, but I fell back on the fact that Leonard had done this hundreds of times.

Then the race official made the final introduction before the race would begin. "Ladies and gentlemen, now I would like to introduce the captain of the host organization for the Tulsa Metro Run this year. Please welcome from the Tulsa Running Team, Dietrich Fulmer."

Applause sounded throughout the crowd of competitors and the spectators who were positioned along the starting line.

I heard Dietrich Fulmer say, "The Tulsa Running Team is proud to be the host organization for the Tulsa Metro Run this year. The Tulsa Metro Run is a sanctioned race. This is important because it allows competitors to qualify their times for future races and allows runners to challenge for positions on competitive teams."

He chuckled conspiratorially and continued. "We actually have a novice runner competing for a position on our own Tulsa Running Team here today."

A murmur drifted throughout the sea of runners. I was glad that no one knew he was talking about me.

Then Dietrich Fulmer concluded with words I will never forget as long as I live. "Finally, ladies and gentlemen, this is the 25th Annual Tulsa Metro Run. Since it has always been run along the exact same course, our team—as the host for this event—has exercised our prerogative to make a slight alteration in the route to commemorate the quarter century of this wonderful competition."

I felt cold steel pierce my heart.

Dietrich Fulmer laughed maniacally as muttered questions echoed throughout the runners.

"Don't worry, folks. It's the same course along the river that you've all come to expect. We've only changed three simple turns just before the finish line to give today's competition some excitement. So may the best runner win."

Cold sweat poured down my body. All of my hopes and dreams, along with months and miles of effort, flushed down the drain.

The dream of Leonard Ryan and me running together, and me actually beating Viktor Fulmer had just gone from unlikely to unthinkable.

Predictably, Leonard said, "It won't be a problem."

I shot back with anger, frustration, and rage, "Yeah, it won't be a problem 'cause we're getting out of here."

I heard the voices of runners around us. "Hey, this is for runners only." "Did somebody order a penguin?" And "You're not supposed to be here."

Then I recognized a familiar voice as the runners nearest to Leonard and me parted.

"Jacob, me boy. Today's the day we've been waiting for," Sister Mary Florene proclaimed excitedly.

I blurted, "Sister, this isn't going to work. I mean, we're not going to..."

She laughed as if she hadn't heard what I had said and stated, "Just before ye take off here, I have something for ye."

She laughed and continued, "You're going to have to bend forward a bit as I'm not the tallest nun in the convent."

Without thinking, I did as ordered and bent forward, and she slipped something around my neck and explained, "Now, Jacob, that is a medal commemorating St. Sebastian. He is the patron saint of athletes, and he'll be running with you as you cross the finish line as a winner."

I cried, "I can't do this. You don't understand."

She reached up and patted my shoulder and said, "I understand better than you think. We're going to need a bit of help in a few areas, but if you'll just worry about doing all you can do, the rest will be taken care of."

The voice on the loud speaker was announcing the runners in our start group.

Leonard said, "Jake, it's now or never."

Truer words were never spoken.

Chapter Forty Five

Simple plans are the best ones; however, there are times when the situation calls for a lot of elements to be put into play at once. The plan I was getting ready to light the fuse on had a lot of moving parts, but I have found over the years when I just do all that I can do, somehow the rest hopefully falls into place.

This was in my mind late that afternoon when I alerted Franklin that kickoff time had arrived. We walked out of Mrs. Balfour's house, down the front porch steps, and over to Monica's car. Franklin opened the passenger door for me, and I slid in. He closed the door and moved around to the side of the house facing away from the ridge.

Then, just as we had planned, I heard three shots fired in rapid succession. They shattered the silence and echoed across the valley and up the ridge. Then, two minutes later, I heard the trunk of Monica's car open and slam shut just before Franklin opened the driver's side door and slid behind the wheel.

A brief rumble signaled all was in order.

I placed two short phone calls on my cell phone in quick succession and then rolled down the passenger window to wait and listen.

In a little less than six minutes, according to my Braille watch, a siren could be heard in the distance. I nodded to Franklin. He immediately started Monica's car, and we backed down the driveway and moved rapidly along the country road.

We were less than a mile from Mrs. Balfour's property when a Perkins sheriff's cruiser, with sirens screaming, passed us at a high rate of speed.

Franklin drove us into downtown Perkins and backed Monica's car into a space on Main Street between two large pickup trucks that afforded a view of the sheriff's office while keeping us relatively concealed.

Franklin got out and walked down the sidewalk and entered a store. It was just a few minutes before he returned and got back into the driver's side of Monica's car.

We sat and waited.

Waiting can be the most difficult but important part of the lost and found business. It's not so much the fact that you have to just sit around and wait. It's the fact that you're never sure what you expect to happen is really going to happen when the wait is over.

This time, we only had to wait a few minutes before the siren of the sheriff's car could be heard in the distance, rapidly approaching. It screeched to a halt in front of the sheriff's office.

Franklin rumbled and announced, "Sir, it seems that two of Perkins' finest have taken Cleve Grovner into custody. They are escorting him into the sheriff's office, and it appears he is wearing a pair of handcuffs."

It was barely four more minutes when Franklin sniffed and proclaimed, "Sir, Walter Grovner is hurriedly walking down the sidewalk toward the sheriff's office. It appears he is in a bit of a foul mood."

We gave Walter Grovner a couple of minutes to get into the sheriff's office. Then I signaled Franklin, and he pulled Monica's car across Main Street and parked it directly in front of the sheriff's office.

I said, "Well, it's now or never."

Franklin rumbled, and we got out of the car and made our way into the front door of the sheriff's office. As we entered, we were met with the sounds of angry shouting and chaos.

Franklin and I stood still until someone finally noticed us. The office went dead silent, and I heard the voice of Sheriff Oliver Shaw say, "I didn't expect to see you two here. You boys are under arrest."

Deputies rushed behind Franklin and me and snapped handcuffs on our wrists. We were escorted into the tiny conference room that was already overheated and overcrowded. Franklin steered me to a chair, and the two of us sat quietly.

The sheriff barked, "Read them their rights."

One of the deputies began reciting, "You have the right to remain silent."

I interrupted. "Franklin's pretty good at remaining silent, but it's not my strong suit."

The deputy paid no attention to my interruption and continued, "You have the right to an attorney, and if you cannot afford one, one will be appointed..."

I interrupted again. "Oh, don't worry. We got an attorney, and he's on the way."

I spoke confidently, but deep down, I hoped it was true.

The sheriff silenced everyone and spoke. "I had a feeling you guys were gonna be trouble. What have you got to say for yourselves?"

Just as I was trying to think of a response to his question, I heard the outer door to the sheriff's office open, and one of the deputies in the entryway spoke.

"Who are you? You can't go in there. I'm a deputy sheriff."

I heard the voice of Clifford Melville say, "I don't care if you're the Queen Mother. I'm the attorney general of the State of Tennessee, and I'm going in there."

And he did.

Chapter Forty Six

Leonard and I shuffled forward toward the starting line. I was in a daze, and my feet seemed to be moving automatically.

I heard a runner behind me and off to my right shout, "Hey, lady, you can't..."

Then, before I knew it, Monica slipped into my arms and kissed me. She said, "Jake, listen. I know everything's a little messed up right now, but if you'll just run your race, I'll work out the details and fill you in at the mid-race water station."

I simply shrugged, trying to think of something to say when she said, "Jacob Dyer, trust me."

She kissed me again and was gone.

I had already trusted her a million times, and Monica had never let me down. So when the starting line official signaled it was our turn, Leonard simply ordered, "Let's go."

And that's what we did.

I tried to block out the swarming horde of runners that surrounded me and the chaotic shouts from the spectators.

Leonard and I were struggling to find a comfortable rhythm to our stride when I heard the voice of Viktor Fulmer on my right.

He began mocking us by singing a variation of *three blind mice, see how they run.*

I laughed as if it didn't matter and called out, "Viktor, it must have taken you weeks to come up with that."

But deep down, it affected me. It also must have affected Leonard, because I felt a tug on the phone cord, and we moved ahead in tandem with a confident stride and a speed we had never run before.

The first few miles went by in a blur. Leonard had been right when he told me the adrenaline of race day would allow us to run faster than we had ever done in training.

I was just beginning to feel a slight bit of hope in my spirit as Leonard and I clicked off the miles at a competitive pace when I remembered that there was no way that I could finish this race. Somewhere in the middle of downtown, with about a quarter of a mile to go, I was going to drop into a black hole of nothingness.

The many days and hours of practice on the original race route meant nothing. I was thinking how unfair it all was when I remembered that life had never been fair to me—or anyone else, for that matter.

I placed my hope, as I had done so many times, in Monica.

I was shocked when Leonard alerted me that we would be approaching the halfway watering station shortly.

The race organizers had set up a massive watering station with cups and dispensers for all the runners to use. The more serious competitors had friends or team members standing by at the edge of the race course to hand them bottles of water so they could keep running without breaking stride.

Leonard announced, "Monica is coming up on your right."

I held out my right hand, and Monica put a bottle of water into it and passed one to Leonard as she said, "Jacob, there are three turns. Just remember eleven o'clock, two o'clock, and ten o'clock."

Leonard and I resumed our pace and merged back into the rapidly flowing river of runners. Monica fell away behind us, and the slight bit of hope I felt earlier returned to me.

I heard the desperation in Leonard's voice as he asked, "What in the world is she talking about?"

I barked out a laugh and responded, "It's a really complicated system. The only thing you need to do is to get me to the first turn, even with Viktor Fulmer."

He questioned, "And then what are *you* going to do, Jacob?"

I responded with the confidence I wish I felt. "I'm going to trust in Monica, trust the system, and beat that worm."

Viktor Fulmer continued taunting us and running alongside Leonard and me, and then rapidly moving into the lead. I knew we needed to pick up the pace and push him harder before Leonard released me for the last quarter mile sprint on my own.

Leonard was laboring beside me but keeping a steady pace. Fulmer seemed to be running effortlessly, and I knew I needed to do something.

Everyone thinks that blind people have great hearing. I don't know that I hear any better than anyone else, but I certainly listen more carefully.

As Viktor Fulmer rushed ahead of us again, I turned to Leonard and said, "Don't let it bother you. I've never thought of you that way, and I don't care what Viktor Fulmer says."

Leonard shot back, "I didn't hear him. What did he say?"

I responded, "Oh, it was just something about you being an old, broken down, three-legged turtle."

I felt the tension in the phone cord as Leonard found a new gear, and we moved ahead rapidly.

Over the next few miles, Viktor Fulmer struggled to keep up with us. When Leonard told me we were two miles from our disconnect point, I thought one more imaginary insult from Viktor Fulmer might just get us there in perfect position.

I said, "Leonard, I think you'll get there just fine, and I don't think Viktor knows what he's talking about when he says you have a weak stride and a pathetic pace."

Once again, the phone cord pulled taut, and I knew we had a chance. My rough calculations told me that Leonard Ryan was getting about three miles to the insult.

Chapter Forty Seven

Clifford Melville stood in the doorway of the cramped room and took charge.

He said, "I'm Clifford Melville. I know Jacob Dyer here, and this must be his colleague Franklin."

I heard a rumble beside me and Franklin said, "It's nice to meet you, sir. You'll forgive me for not shaking your hand as these cuffs seem to have me a bit encumbered."

The sheriff announced, "I'm Sheriff Oliver Shaw, and this is my office."

Clifford responded, "Yes, sir, I know it's your office, but I'm the attorney general, and it's my state. But just relax. We're on the same side here."

Walter Grovner shouted, "I object. You can't be the attorney general and represent Dyer at the same time."

Clifford laughed derisively and said, "Well, if it isn't old Whip Lash Walter—the cellar dweller of my law school class. I heard you liked the bar exam so well you took it three times. Or was it four?"

Walter Grovner sputtered, "I'm a duly licensed attorney, here representing my brother Cleve Grovner."

Cleve stood so abruptly he knocked his chair over backwards and cried, "Look, I already told you. I threatened the old lady, burned her barn, and shot her dog and a couple of cows, but..."

Walter hissed, "Shut up, Cleve!"

Cleve continued, "I didn't kill the old lady, and I'm not going to take the fall for this and get the death penalty."

Clifford Melville clapped his hands and silenced everyone.

"Listen, how do we know that anybody got killed?"

Sheriff Shaw explained, "Our office received an anonymous tip, relayed from the receptionist at the Baptist Church, telling us that shots had been fired at Mrs. Lucinda Balfour's home, and she may be dead.

Clifford asked, "Do you get a lot of tips from the Baptist Church?"

The sheriff answered, "Look. The receptionist from the church called and said someone phoned in the tip and hung up, so I sent two deputies out to see what happened, and they found Cleve Grovner wandering around the property."

Cleve stamped his foot and said, "I was outside my trailer on my own property when I heard some shots down there. Then I could see this Limey flunky of Dyer's loading a body into the trunk of the sports car."

Franklin's prolonged sniff expressed his opinion of Cleve Grovner as Grovner continued, "When the car drove off, I walked down to see what was going on when the deputies showed up, slapped the cuffs on me, and brought me in."

Clifford asked, "So then you called your brother and asked him to come over here?"

The sheriff stated, "He hasn't called anyone yet."

Clifford inquired, "So, Walter, how did you come to be here at this little tea party?"

Walter whined, "I was just sitting in my office, minding my own business, when some reporter called to ask if I would be defending my brother against any murder charges he might be facing that would result in the death penalty."

Clifford Melville turned his attention to Franklin and asked, "Franklin, did you shoot anybody?"

Franklin sniffed and replied, "No, sir. I merely discharged my weapon three times, shooting at a target beside Mrs. Balfour's home. I like to keep in practice, you know."

Clifford said, "Yes, I know. Did you hit the target?"

"Most assuredly, sir. Three times," Franklin reported.

"Jacob," Clifford asked me, "is there a body in the trunk of that car?"

I sounded as innocent as a newborn babe as I answered, "Not to my knowledge."

He inquired, "Well, then, would you voluntarily allow one of the sheriff's men to look in the trunk?"

"Absolutely," I responded.

A very young and nervous deputy fumbled the car keys out of Franklin's jacket pocket and left the room. He returned in less than a minute and stammered as if he had seen a ghost.

"Sheriff, I opened it up a crack, and there's a body laying in there, so I just slammed it shut and figured we'd ought to wait for the medical examiner."

My friend Clifford Melville questioned me. "Jacob, what about it?"

I resumed my innocent tone and said, "I don't see how it's even possible for there to be a body in the trunk of Monica's sports car. You see, the trunk is so small that after Franklin laid the scarecrow in there, I don't even think you could get as much as a brief case in, much less a body."

The sheriff yelled at his deputy, "Son, give me those car keys."

The sheriff stomped out of the room and returned almost immediately.

He settled back into his chair and said, "Well, there isn't a body in there, but I would like to hear Franklin's explanation as to why he's driving around with a scarecrow in the trunk."

Franklin rumbled, cleared his throat, and began. "Yes, sir. As you may well know, Mr. Dyer and I have been staying on the property as guests of Mrs. Balfour, a lovely woman, who keeps an immaculate house and tends a wonderful garden.

"In her absence, as time has permitted, I have tried to keep up with the chores in her garden, and the scarecrow has really bothered me."

The sheriff's tone was measured as he tried to remain calm. "And can you tell us why this scarecrow bothered you?"

Franklin continued. "Yes, sir. I noticed as we first arrived that this particular scarecrow was rather rumpled and disheveled. Actually, he was altogether disreputable-looking. So I told Mr Dyer, when we had an opportunity, I would like to find more suitable attire for the scarecrow."

The sheriff was at the edge of his patience as he asked, "So why is the scarecrow in the trunk?"

Franklin rumbled and responded, "Well, sir, we brought him into town because I had noticed a thrift store on your main street here and thought, when the opportunity presented itself, I would see what might be available that would both look appropriate and fit the scarecrow in question."

The sheriff slapped the table, and Clifford Melville laughed and asked, "So, did you find anything for the scarecrow?"

Franklin gave a hearty rumble and announced, "Most assuredly, sir. I located a moss green tuxedo—what I believe you Yanks would call a lounge lizard suit. It's not something that a proper gentleman would wear ordinarily, but I felt that the moss green would be very fitting in the garden, and the sequined lapel will be ideal for frightening away any predatory birds."

Cleve Grovner shouted angrily, "So what did you do with the body?"

I responded meekly, "Well, unless something has happened to her in the last hour or so, I think you could find Mrs. Lucinda Balfour at the Trail's End Resort."

The sheriff ordered one of the deputies. "Make the call."

The deputy scurried out of the room and was back in a minute or two, stating, "She's there, sir."

Walter Grovner laughed uncomfortably and said, "Well, I guess it's all just a big misunderstanding, and we can all go home."

Clifford Melville spoke in a tone worthy of the attorney general of the great State of Tennessee.

"Not so fast. We have several issues here.

"First, Cleve Grovner, I believe you have admitted to firing a rifle—which is a violation of your parole—and should make you a guest of the state for the remaining 12 years of your original manslaughter sentence.

"On top of that, you've admitted to shooting Mrs. Balfour's dog and her cows as well as burning her barn. If you put those charges on top of the original sentence you're already facing, I think you're going to be with us for a long time."

Cleve Grovner roared, "I thought I was facing the death penalty. I wouldn't have admitted to it except..."

The sheriff interrupted and ordered a deputy, "Let's find a cell for Mr. Grovner here."

There was a brief scuffle as the deputy led Cleve Grovner out of the room.

Walter Grovner declared, "That won't stand up. He's been framed. I can get him off in a heartbeat."

Clifford Melville declared, "Oh, I believe it will hold up, but you won't be getting anybody off on anything. My office got one of those anonymous tip phone calls, too, and, Walter, we've been checking into your inappropriate dealings on the parole board—particularly as they relate to your brother—and this unsavory business involving you being on the highway commission."

Walter coughed but was unable to speak.

Clifford continued, "Well, Walter, it's not all bad. You won't be able to represent Cleve, but I think you will be able to keep him company for a lot of years in the penitentiary."

The sheriff ordered, "Somebody find a cell for this other Grovner, too. And get the cuffs off of Mr. Dyer and his colleague."

A few minutes later, Franklin and I were standing on the sidewalk outside the sheriff's office with Clifford Melville.

He shook hands with Franklin and me and said, "Jake, Walter Grovner was actually right when he said I couldn't be your lawyer while I am serving as the attorney general."

I laughed and said, "It sounds like it may have been the only legal opinion Walter ever got right."

Clifford joined in the laughter and said, "Well, you don't owe me a legal fee, but I at least think I ought to get a dinner."

The Sound of Victory

Chapter Forty Eight

The roar of the spectators increased as the Tulsa Metro Run funneled into downtown. The shouts and cheers echoed from the concrete, steel, and glass buildings.

The knot in my stomach pulled tighter as Leonard and I rapidly ran toward the designated point where I was to disconnect from my umbilical cord that safely attached me to Leonard's wrist and, more importantly, his eyes.

Viktor Fulmer was laboring heavily as he ran right beside me.

Leonard said, between his heavy breaths, "About a half mile 'til we separate, partner. Let's show this jerk how real runners finish a race."

I was quite certain Leonard Ryan had not run that fast in the late stage of a race for many years. He gave me everything he had, and I knew that if I didn't beat Viktor Fulmer, it wasn't going to be Leonard's fault.

Leonard's stride faltered as he staggered the last few yards toward our prearranged release point.

As I slipped the knotted phone cord from around my wrist, Leonard stumbled to the pavement and shouted, "Eleven o'clock, Jake... now!"

Viktor Fulmer yelled, "I've got you now, blind man. You don't have a chance."

I couldn't answer him. It took every ounce of my concentration to focus directly toward eleven o'clock. The thunderous roar and the chaos of the runners swirling about me was a living thing. I was floating free in the middle of the universe with no point of perspective.

I did the only thing I could do, and ran.

I ran for John Ivers who had saved my life in Vietnam and lost his own life when we got home. I ran for Leonard Ryan who had gotten me to

177

this point and deserved to win this race. I ran for Monica who had given me the whole world. And, finally, I ran for Jacob Dyer, because I wanted to show the whole world and myself that I wasn't a loser.

I sprinted forward like a ship without a compass or a rudder. I trusted in Monica's words, but I couldn't imagine how I could make this work. I knew, at some point, I would have to make a turn toward two o'clock.

Just as I was about to give up hope, I heard a shrill, piercing whistle from the direction of two o'clock. I had heard that same whistle only once before, but I couldn't forget it, so I turned immediately and ran directly toward Sister Mary Florene.

Viktor Fulmer was still running right beside me, but I knew we were both at the very edge of our speed and endurance. I blocked out his taunts and the intensifying crowd noise and waited for the last signal that I hoped I would hear and recognize.

A Rolls Royce is a magnificent automobile. It costs more than most people pay for their house, so I would not have ever ridden in one except for a little old lady named Maude Henson who was heir to an immense oil fortune. After the Dyer Straits Lost and Found Agency had successfully resolved a matter for Maude, she gave me the use of Franklin and that marvelous car.

The Rolls Royce has an incomparable engine that can purr quietly while performing like a race car. It has a sumptuous interior that makes you feel like you're sitting in the throne room of a palace. And it has a distinctive horn that sounds as if it's coming from a distant lighthouse on a rocky, fog-shrouded shore.

I heard that unmistakable sound calling to me from my left at precisely the ten o'clock position, and I made the final turn for home.

Viktor Fulmer was still right beside me, but his breathing was becoming ragged, and I could feel his doubt and frustration building.

When I was in basic training, I had a drill instructor who told me, "When you think you've given it all, you haven't."

Over the last few yards of the Tulsa Metro Run on that day, even my drill instructor would have admitted that Private Dyer gave it all.

I had no idea where the finish line was, but then I heard the unmistakable voice of Monica shout, "Jacob, lean forward... now!"

I took one more step and leaned forward. I could hear yells and screams as the whole world fell away.

There were vaguely familiar sounds and smells just below the surface of my consciousness. Part of me wanted to know where I was and what was happening, but another part of me simply wanted to float in the void.

I broke through the surface of consciousness when I heard a familiar voice say, "Jacob, me boy, you've got a bit of a concussion but nothing serious. After all, it's only your head. Here we are again in the exact same room in the hospital in the middle of the night. The Mother Superior is starting to wonder what I am doing gallivanting about at all hours."

She laughed and continued, "Well, it gives her and the sisters something to talk about."

I croaked, "What happened?"

"Well, Jacob," she explained, "probably the best way to summarize it is to quote from the front page of the early edition of this morning's *Tulsa World*. Beneath the banner headline that says *Midnight Runner Wins*, there's a wonderful photo of you, Jacob."

I heard the paper rustle and she stepped closer to my bed.

"The picture shows Viktor Fulmer at the finish line of the race. The only thing in front of him is your nose, your chin, and a dangling Saint Sebastian medal commemorating the blessed patron saint of athletes."

"I won?" I asked.

Sister Mary Florene said, "Jake, I told you if you just do the best you can do, the rest will be taken care of."

I declared, "Well, sister, I did the best I could."

She replied, "Yes, Jacob, you sure did."

I said reverently, "Sister, I'd appreciate it if you'd kinda thank your boss. You know, The Big Guy, for me."

Sister Mary Florene said, "Already done, me boy. Now, get some sleep."

Chapter Forty Nine

A lot of people celebrate the new year at the stroke of midnight on January 1ˢᵗ freezing to death while watching a ball drop with thousands of other intoxicated revelers in New York's Times Square. Millions of other people celebrate the new year by watching those same festivities on network television.

I have always thought this was sad, because these misguided people simply fail to understand that the new year begins on the opening day of baseball season.

As usual, my radio was tuned in to the beloved St. Louis Cardinals' game as they were, once again, battling the godless Chicago Cubs on the hallowed ground of the new stadium in St. Louis.

I had an ice-cold beer in my hand and a magnificent cigar from Guatemala burning vigorously.

The Cubs went down in order with three quick outs in the top of the first inning, and then you could feel the excitement building as the first Cardinal batter of the year strode toward the plate and stepped into the batter's box.

The St. Louis radio broadcaster painted the picture. "Well, fans, the grass is green, the sky is blue, and the Cardinals are red. It doesn't get any better than this. The Cubs hurler winds up, and the pitch is on the way."

You could hear the bat crack as the announcer described, "That's a hot foul ball, headed into the stands above the dugout on the first base side."

I could actually hear the fans in the stands scream and yell as the ball rocketed toward them. Shouts of "Look out!" could be heard as the baseball bounced in the aisle, grazed my left thigh, and plopped into my lap. I grabbed the ball in my right hand and held it over my head triumphantly.

The radio announcer proclaimed, "Well, Card fans, it's taken over 40 years, but now I've seen it all. Jacob Dyer is a longtime Cardinals' fan who faithfully listens to the Cardinal games on these radio broadcasts. But, today, Jake and his party are guests of the Cardinals' management, and they're in the box seats right behind first base.

"Jacob Dyer is a blind guy, and he actually caught that foul ball, ladies and gentlemen. I'll tell you, sports fans, when a blind guy can make a catch like that on one hop in the first inning on opening day, it's got to be a good omen that we're going to have a great season here in St. Louis."

The opening day game and the weekend three-game series with the Chicago Cubs was a celebration that Monica, Franklin, and I had been planning for quite some time. Monica's grandmother, Lucinda Balfour, had joined us in St. Louis, and she was sitting right behind Monica.

After Cleve and Walter Grovner had headed off to prison for the foreseeable future, Monica had helped her grandmother make arrangements to have the ramshackle trailer and all of the garbage cleared away from her land on top of the ridge.

The highway project had just been announced, and Mrs. Balfour had received a ridiculous amount of money for one small corner of her property, but the highway wouldn't disturb the old house that had been in the family for generations or her prized garden with the garish tuxedo-clad scarecrow presiding over everything.

Mrs. Balfour had struck up a fascinating personal and professional relationship with Leonard Ryan, who had joined us for the baseball weekend in St. Louis. Leonard was helping Monica's grandmother plan how to invest and shelter her highway money while enjoying getting to know an amazing old lady.

After the Tulsa Metro Run, I—with Leonard as my sighted guide—had become the eighth member of the Tulsa Running Team, displacing

Viktor Fulmer. We had run a few small races together, but when Leonard decided to retire, I told the team's captain, Dietrich Fulmer, I would give his brother Viktor his slot on the team back under one condition. It was unanimously agreed that Leonard Ryan would be named Captain Emeritus and lifetime coach of the Tulsa Running Team.

All of us enjoyed the game thoroughly, even though the Cardinals were trailing 3 to 2 in the bottom of the ninth with a man on 3rd base.

Just as if the baseball gods were working overtime, the stadium announcer proclaimed, "Next batter, number 5, Cardinal first baseman, Albert Pujols."

The crowd went wild, anticipating another one of Albert's game-winning home runs.

But, alas, the stars were not aligned perfectly that day, and Albert didn't hit a homerun; however, he did knock a double off of the right field wall which scored the tying run. Then Albert stole third and scored the winning run by sliding under the catcher's tag on a wild pitch.

Sometimes when life doesn't go like you planned, you find out that it's better than you expected.

As we walked out of the stadium arm-in-arm and strolled toward the St. Louis arch and the riverfront, Monica asked, "Jake, how did you catch that ball?"

"It's magic," I answered.

We walked a while in silence, then Monica whispered softly, "I didn't know about magic until I met you."

I whispered back, "The magic didn't show up in my life until you did."

CPSIA information can be obtained
at www.ICGtesting.com
Printed in the USA
FFOW02n1956071214
9248FF